THE GOD DRUG

THE GOD DRUG

Book One of the Posthuman series

MIKAEL SVANSTRÖM

This is a work of fiction. Names, characters, businesses, places, events and incidents are either the products of the author's imagination or used in a fictitious manner. Any resemblance to actual persons, living or dead, or actual events is purely coincidental.

1st Edition
Copyright © 2015 Mikael Svanstrom
All Rights Reserved

Edited by: Don Ellis
Cover design: Denis Lenzi

ISBN: 978-0-6488549-2-0

To Marcus Sigurdsson:

Thanks!

A Clash of Titans

"Why are you following me?"

Tom stopped, surprised that Elize had chosen to confront him. He had been lazy, as he suspected she'd known he was following her all along. What piqued his interest was why she had chosen this time to confront him.

Her eyes focused on him for an instant and then returned to gazing into the distance. He knew why – when he was amped up he did the same. The physical aspect of human beings didn't generate enough information to remain interesting for more than a second or two.

"You have 30 seconds. Why are you following me?"

He knew she had already calculated all his answers. He briefly wondered what probability she had assigned the truth.

"I've been hired by PharmaCom to bring you in," he said. "Thought I'd follow you to figure out the best way to do it."

He could see she wasn't surprised. He had just confirmed one of the many possible paths leading to another set of calculated choices.

"You won't stop me now," she said, and turned to walk towards the bank building across the road.

So much for my 30 seconds, Tom thought, and hurried after her.

"Don't do it," he shouted. "He's in there."

She didn't acknowledge the warning. In all likelihood it was the reason she was going there. Tom stopped and watched her walk through traffic as if it didn't exist, fascinated by her fluidity, every movement calculated to perfection. He considered following her, but knew there was little he could do inside the building. He would more than likely be caught in the crossfire. Better to wait outside until one of them reappeared.

Tom had been following her for the past two weeks. This was the third time she had visited what seemed to be a random place to meet Adrian, who he now thought of as the Adversary. He was no closer to understanding what she was doing than when he had started. He had begun to regret taking the job, but didn't have the luxury of declining good-paying jobs. Nowadays, people left digital traces if they so much as sneezed. Most cases could be solved by techs from the comfort of their chairs, so he couldn't be too picky.

Three minutes later an explosion inside the building sent glass flying in a deadly spray. Chunks of reinforced concrete followed, turning the sidewalk into an abattoir. A sudden windfall of green lights had let the heavy traffic gain momentum and it was now hit by the scattershot of metal and stone. Tom watched as death appeared in front of him.

Time slowed down. He knew he was having an episode, but had no way of preventing his mind from going into freefall. Tom sat down on the ground and let it wash over him. The carnage took on a pattern, unfolding like a rose opening up in slow motion. He watched the mathematical precision of the pile-up as it dominoed from ground zero in all directions, metal bending into new shapes far more fascinating than the smooth lines it originally had.

The collective blaring of car horns and alarms brought him back to the reality of the situation. He was glad to see he had only been out for fifteen seconds at most. Since he had quit using IntelEz, this had happened five times. Recently, a so-called friend had sent him a repeating fractal video. He had sat staring at it for two hours until mental exhaustion had blurred his vision enough for him to snap out of it.

No one could have survived the blast, not even Elize, but he still wanted to make sure. He climbed over the hood of a car and jumped to another one, when the shockwave from a second explosion left him sprawled on the ground. It was followed by a groan from the building itself as the supporting structure bent out of shape.

He didn't care. Once he had started getting episodes, he knew he didn't have long and he had to see this to the end. He stood up and continued towards the building, glass crunching under his shoes. He entered the bank through the gaping hole that had been a glassed-in entry hall. Another groan from the building was followed by debris falling from the floors above. A middle-aged woman walked past him in a daze. She had a large cut across her face, but otherwise looked uninjured. It gave him some hope to see someone alive, but he knew the two people he was looking for would have been close to ground zero.

The entrance led to a high-ceilinged open area. The walls were cracked, exposing the support structure. Steel beams buckled out like giant spider legs, threatening to give way at any moment. Two floors above had caved into the middle of the open area, creating a mountain of unstable debris. The blast had originated further inside the building. To get there, Tom had no choice but to brave the precarious structure. He was halfway up when he heard noises on the other side and felt movement in the rubble he was standing on. Someone trying to scale the structure on the other side had upset its internal balance. Tom stood still, willing the large pieces of masonry above him to fall inwards. It started shifting before an avalanche of debris fell away from him and buried whoever had been there. It was a miracle he was still standing.

Tom jumped from island to island until he reached the other side. He guessed this was the secure area next to where customers came in to visit the bank. Two corridors led to the back of the bank. Metal from the reinforced walls was twisted outwards from the blast. This must have been where the blast originated. Tom looked into the gaping hole and to his surprise saw movement. A shape was making its way through the scorched remains of the metal boxes in the vault. He ducked down and watched as the shape came into the light.

The man was a mess – blackened and bloodied, walking with a limp and cradling one of his arms. The most disturbing aspect of the man was not his appearance. It was the coughing sound that Tom could only translate as laughter. He knew who it was, even with the disfiguring wounds and raw, hairless scalp. Adrian rivalled any A-list celebrity in publicity, even if he had been out of the press lately. He had been the poster boy for the Drug for over a year until the long-term side effects made it illegal.

"Help me," Adrian commanded, staring at the place where Tom huddled. Tom stood up and nodded towards Adrian, who repeated his command. Tom hesitated – Elize might still be in there. If Adrian was alive perhaps she was too.

"You came for her," Adrian said, a statement of fact, not a question. "She is dead. I need your help. You will help me."

"You survived," Tom said.

"I came prepared."

Tom hesitated. He still wanted to confirm Elize's death with his own eyes.

"Her body is in there," Adrian said. "Just hurry. I will not make it out of here on my own before the police arrive and your employer wouldn't like it if you missed an opportunity to bring me in."

Tom shook his head and made his way to the blackened metal jaw, barely able to avoid the ragged edges. He had no idea how Adrian knew anything about his employer, but he was right. His contract stated quite clearly that either Adrian or Elize was an acceptable target. Tom didn't have time to join the dots. Adrian had been right about the timing too. Soon there would be police and fire brigades swarming the place.

He made his way through the corridor. The blast, or at least one of them, had originated in the vault, funnelling out through the corridor into the main hall. The explosion had shredded the metal storage boxes and vaporised most of their contents. The ceiling was gone, opening a gash in the building four levels high. Not even the enormous vault door had withstood the blast. It had been ripped from its hinges and was lodged halfway into the opposite wall. A charred body lay in the middle of the corridor, just outside the vault. It was still relatively intact, which seemed impossible considering the force of the explosion. Debris fell from the floors above, hitting the floor around him. He didn't have time to check for vital signs. She was most surely dead. He took a sample from the body with a penknife and put it in a plastic ziplock bag.

"We have to go," Adrian yelled, followed by coughing attack.

Tom turned to leave and for the briefest of moments thought he saw movement. He turned and stared at the body, willing it to move again, before convincing himself he was mistaken. A chair and then a desk crashed to the floor next to him, and he knew it was time to leave.

"Now!"

Tom hurried back down the corridor and caught up with Adrian, who was making his way slowly across the large hall. Police had already arrived outside and officers were busy closing off the area. Tom picked Adrian up and carried him out of the building. A police officer greeted them outside.

"Is he ok? Are you ok?"

"I'm fine," Adrian said and smiled. "Help the others. I'm fine with my friend here."

"Any more live ones?" he asked, staring at the devastation.

"On the upper floors perhaps," Tom said.

"Ambulances are on the way. You can wait over there." He indicated an area close to the intersection. They both watched the police officer hurry off. Tom headed in the general direction the officer had indicated, but as soon as no one was watching, he hurried down a side street.

"Put me down," Adrian said. He already seemed more mobile than before, his breathing no longer laboured.

"No, you're coming with me."

Adrian just nodded, and Tom carried him another block. He was aiming for his car parked a few blocks away.

"You took a sample of her body," Adrian said. "It won't do you any good."

"I've got you. I don't need a sample."

"When did you give it up?"

Tom knew what he referred to, even if he hadn't said it.

"A month ago."

"Do you have episodes?"

Tom didn't answer. He didn't have to. He was sure Adrian already knew the answer.

"I wish you'd put me down," Adrian said finally.

Tom, tired from carrying Adrian, complied. A blinding flash and Tom was suddenly weightless, lifting at first, and then falling forward in a heap. Engulfing pain and darkness followed.

2

The Drug

Shapes emerged as light patches against dark shades. Patterns superimposed on the shapes slowly gained coherence. With consciousness came pulsating flashes of pain, emanating from the base of his skull. He had been struck in the back of the head with some kind of blunt weapon. He had no idea how long he'd been out.

Tom blinked and felt alive for the first time since he'd come off the Drug. The pain sliced through the sluggishness of thought and brought clarity. He knew what the Drug did. Once the long-term side effects became apparent, little else was seen as newsworthy. It hyper-charged your capacity for processing data and information – a wonder drug, if there ever was one. The brain immediately responded by allowing more and more input, regardless of source. Once the brain had gotten used to the Drug after years of use, the input level remained, whilst the brain efficiency deteriorated. Pain helped limit the input momentarily.

Tom looked around and was surprised to see Adrian being helped into a black car by two men further down the street. He had no idea who they were. Most likely a rival drug company or a government agency.

He hurried to the street whilst hailing a rent-a-car on his Omni Device. A small electric Tesla A-class stopped almost immediately. Tom loaded a hack into the drive computer, assigned Adrian's car as the lead and let the Assisted Driver Network do its job.

He pulled out a first aid kit from the glove compartment and was immediately informed by the car that the usage would be charged to his account. He accepted and started dabbing the back of his head with an alcowipe. There was hardly any blood. Whoever had struck him had done an expert job – exactly the right amount of force at the precise location to knock him out without causing permanent damage. Or he'd just been lucky.

They entered a downtown area with very little traffic. Tom knew where they were. This was a dead zone. All major cities had areas where they kept people who had deteriorated into a form of autism from the Drug. They were still capable of taking care of their most basic needs, but hardly anything else. Tom knew he had only another couple of years, probably less, before he too would end up here.

A few minutes later the black car stopped. Tom immediately changed the end destination in the drive computer to half a block further down the street, hoping it would be enough to avoid suspicion. He watched as the two men helped Adrian to the front door of a five-story apartment building. Not even with his newfound clarity could Tom make sense of the situation. The two men didn't look like operatives. Even if they were, since when did they operate out of a dead zone? His initial plan had been to follow them into the building, but he decided against it. If it really was a safe house, he could be watched already. He got out of the car and sent it to a couple of programmed stops around the city to muddle up the digital prints it left. He knew he had a few tails and he didn't want them to focus on this address.

Across the street he found a little alleyway where he could remain relatively hidden whilst keeping an eye on the building. He settled in, expecting a long wait, when he saw movement in one of the windows and someone pulling the curtains shut. It could be coincidence, of course, but he didn't think so. He watched for another couple of hours without seeing any movement in the windows, not that he had expected any. A deadhead would never look out the window for fear of the information overload it would cause.

The events of the last few hours replayed in his mind. One thing in particular that kept cropping up was Elize's body. He replayed the moment in his mind when he thought it had moved. With repetition came certainty. It had moved. She was alive. He knew he might still be mistaken, but even if she were dead, her body was hot property. If he could secure it, he'd have bargaining capital.

He stopped one of the food administrators, a young woman with bio-jewels implanted in a tribal pattern under the skin along her cheek, and offered to pay her double, in cash, if she hailed and pre-paid a car from her account. He made sure the car would drop him off at a train station away from his apartment so no one would connect him to this place. He even loaded a fake id tag in his Omni so the train ride back to his apartment laid a different digital trail.

His efforts to keep a low profile didn't matter in the end. A corporate-issue, H-cell Mercedes was parked right outside his apartment block. He knew Mr. Astin would be inside with his two bio-enhanced thugs. He also knew there was no point in running. Mr. Astin was his contact for the current contract after all.

As he approached, the car door opened. Maybe it was the pain that still pulsated in the back of his head making him see more clearly, but suddenly he didn't feel like sharing anything of the recent events. Although he had only spoken briefly to Adrian and Elize, he now felt he was playing a small part in their destiny. Until he worked out exactly what that was, he didn't want to give away too much. He was almost certain he was the only one who knew the details of what had happened, and he didn't want to share that information. Not yet.

One of the well-dressed thugs stepped out. His immaculate dark suit was designed to hide his bulk, but it was only partially successful. It was the kind of size you could only get if you spent hours in the gym every day, or if you had help from fat-burning, muscle-building drugs. Tom was still amused by the fact that after the Drug became readily available, humankind didn't immediately turn to solving world hunger, pollution or curing diseases. Their first priority was to make themselves prettier, stronger and longer living, and the early major developments were in cosmetics and body enhancements. It was all a moot point now, anyway. The Golden Age created by the Drug was over in less than a decade.

Mr. Astin appeared. If his bodyguards were prime specimens, he was anything but. It was as if he'd ended up just below average in all possible aspects. A little bit on the short side, slightly overweight, with a premature receding hairline and a voice pitched just slightly too high.

"Walk with me," he said, and immediately walked off down the street trailed by the two bodyguards.

Tom was tired and annoyed. He despised everything about Mr. Astin and had to supress an urge to ignore him completely. Instead, he hurried to catch up.

"Remind me. Why did I hire you?"

Sam sighed. Mr. Astin had asked him this same question many times before. It was some kind of power play to put people in their places.

"You hired me to track down one of the anomalies."

He used the word anomaly even though the common term used to describe Adrian and Elize was posthuman. He knew his employer preferred anomaly – it made them a mistake, something that wasn't natural instead of something beyond human.

"And?"

"And to either bring them in or inform you about their whereabouts."

Mr. Astin nodded to himself. "Let's get back to that later. I need to know what happened today."

"I managed to locate Elize again this morning and followed her. She and Adrian caught up again. It seems they're taking turns setting traps for each other. I don't know what triggered the two explosions, but my guess is that Adrian set them off on purpose. I was outside the building at the time and lost track of them after that."

"Do you know why they are fighting?"

"Who knows why they do anything," Tom said, but a glance at Mr. Astin was enough to know that answer wouldn't fly. "I think it's a game.

They're playing a high-stakes version of tag for fun. Who knows, next time they might be throwing black holes at each other."

"So you are saying the two smartest people in the world spend all their time trying to kill each other for kicks?"

"That's what it looks like, yes."

"That's what it looks like," Mr. Astin repeated with a grimace, as if to try out the words himself and not liking the taste.

They walked another block in silence.

"Where did you go after the explosion?" Mr. Astin said suddenly.

"I saw an operative outside the bank and decided to follow him," Tom said, knowing they tracked his car through the Assisted Driver Network. "I thought he might have picked up a trace. Didn't seem to be the case though."

"And now you are walking back to your apartment."

"I like my privacy," Tom said and shrugged.

Mr. Astin stopped and motioned for the two thugs to come up next to him. Tom knew he had yet again gone too far. He took a deep breath and turned to Mr. Astin, who looked like a dwarf next to his hired ogre muscle. He had to supress an urge not to smile.

"I don't know who is following me or how they're doing it. I'm not paid to be easy to track. I'm hired to deliver results and I believe I've done that. I don't want those results to be going to the competition."

Mr. Astin gave him a long look. Tom knew he was deciding what to do. Tom was hiding something and he surely knew that, but was it worth trying to extract it? He was betting on still being seen as useful. As long as that was the case, he had some wiggle room.

"Here's the thing. The information you provide us is useless. We're nowhere closer to understanding what they do or what they are planning. This latest stunt means the government has no choice but to act. They'll pick both of them up as soon as they can. So we have to move first."

He nodded towards one of the bodyguards who handed Tom a small stun gun.

"I'm not expecting you to bring them in, but if you could locate either of them again, contact me immediately and we'll take it from there. I no longer care what they do or why they do it. We can work that out once we've secured one of them."

"I don't think it will be that easy, not judging from today," Tom said, ignored the gun.

"Let me worry about that. Use this if you have to."

Tom had seen bulkier versions of the stun gun before. It sprayed a weblike stream of conductive fibres and sent an electric pulse through it. Even someone who could hardly aim was still able to take down multiple attackers with this thing. It spoke volumes that Mr. Astin thought this was the best weapon to equip him with. It was the weapon of choice for someone who couldn't use a weapon that required any skill.

"We're assuming their physical characteristics are still the same as ours, so it should do the trick."

They were almost back at the car when Mr. Astin stopped and reached out his hand.

"If I find you have kept anything from me, however small, you'll join the deadheads sooner than you think."

"A pleasure as always," Tom said and smiled, deliberately not shaking his hand

"As always," Mr. Astin repeated,

Tom watched the three men leave and hurried to his apartment. If Mr. Astin had to come here to find out what was going on, no one else knew anything either. No one would know it was Elize's body until they tried to identify the victims of the blast, so if he was lucky he'd have tonight to secure it.

3

Morgue Attack

Tom still had access to some of the police systems, courtesy of old friendships that remained after he left the force. He checked them now, but could find no trace of Elize's body logged anywhere. Most bodies were identified through their Omni implants or through other serialised body implants.

Five bodies were unidentified from inside the blast radius – two male, one female and two unknowns. From what he had seen, she was more than likely one of the unknowns. The injuries she had sustained were strange. An explosion should have ripped her apart. Instead her body had been whole, but scarred and burned. He hadn't questioned it because Adrian's injuries had been similar but less severe. The little clothing that had survived had fused with her body. He was confident he'd find her if only he could check the bodies.

All bodies were at the morgue. If he wanted more information about their location, he'd have to hack the system holding the data from the morgue, and it was far beyond his skill level. He could use basic pre-built tools and agents, but hacking a system or data source required much more than that.

He opened a two-way feed to bZane, a low-rent hacker he'd used a few other times. He only knew him by his feed id, but as long as he delivered, Tom didn't care.

"Devine. The PI man. You still in business?"

"I need some help. I need to locate a few bodies in the morgue."

"Didn't take you for a necro-lover."

"I need to know where they are."

"Send me their id tags and I'll get to it."

"No id tags. They're unidentified."

"How could they ..." he started, then stopped. "So what do you know?"

"Female, badly burned, from the downtown explosion today."

The feed went quiet. bZane overrode the visual feed with a doctored Roadrunner cartoon, where Wiley Coyote plans always worked. The Roadrunner met its demise many times over the course of the silence.

"Nasty accident. Terrorists?"

"Possibly. Can you do it?"

"Give me an hour."

Tom packed together a small infiltration kit, consisting mainly of surveillance and lock-hacking equipment. He couldn't afford to have bZane helping more than this, so he had to do it the old-fashioned way.

***

An hour later Tom stood outside the morgue, studying the entrance. A nurse and at least one security guard always occupied the front desk, making it nearly impossible as an entryway. Any silent alarms raised would come from there, so as a precaution he decided to place an audio feed. He didn't have time for anything fancy. Instead he walked into the reception with an unsteady swagger.

"I want to see my Uncle Harry!" he said, slurring his speech and stumbling as he reached the desk. He attached a small transmitter under the desk.

"Does he work here?" the nurse behind the desk asked. She was in her twenties, with dark hair and black make-up; reprogrammable tattoos snaked up her arms. She glanced at one of the guards with an almost imperceptible shake of her head.

"Of course not! He died yesterday."

"Sorry, but that won't happen. I can direct you to a good medium though."

"I don't care about that! He borrowed my nice watch! He was wearing it when he died. I want it back."

Tom slammed his hand in the desk and as he did, attached a clear microphone sticker on the desk right in front of the nurse. She laughed nervously and nodded to the guard.

"Yeah, good luck with that. His effects will be released together with the body. Talk to the funeral parlour."

The guards approached and grabbed him by the arm.

"I'm sorry, officer," Tom said and patted him on the shoulder, again attaching a sticker. "It was a really nice watch. Harry was an ass though."

The guard led him out of the building and left him with a detailed explanation of what would happen to him if he tried to re-enter. As soon as the guard left, Tom routed the sound through his Omni to test the sound quality from the microphones.

"Who wears watches anymore, anyway?" he heard the guard say.

The nurse at the front desk laughed in response.

It worked perfectly. Now he needed to find another way in. There would be roof access and some kind of back door. He checked the back door first and was lucky – it was an old design based on Near Field Communication. Lucky he preferred the old Omni models that still had much of the old functionality of the Smart phones they had replaced. It could act as the identity and a sensor would read its id tag.

Tom attached a key logger to the door and waited. Thirty minutes later a middle-aged man in a hurry exited the morgue and entered a waiting car. Tom checked the contents of the key logger. He had a full copy of the id tag. He loaded it into a clean Omni and as he approached the door there was an audible click. He had expected it to work, but still felt a rush from the success.

He knew he was woefully unprepared for this break-in and that it would take a lot of luck for it to succeed.

"The devil loves a gambling man," he said to himself, as he pulled the door open and strode in with confidence. He had only a vague idea of where he was heading, but knew his best bet was to act as if he knew where he was going. bZane had had the bodies put in a cool room in the basement, so he headed for the stairs. He hoped they hadn't started an autopsy, but it was questionable if they would do one anyway as the cause of death was so obvious.

A male nurse came walking his way. Tom caught his eye, nodded and kept walking.

"Good evening," Tom heard in his earpiece from the reception area. "I'm here to assess the bodies that came in from the explosion earlier today."

Tom had hoped for some more time, but if he was lucky this was just a fishing expedition. They could have noticed a change in data patterns around Elize online and were now checking all possible avenues.

"Sign here and here," the receptionist replied.

Tom ran the rest of the way down the stairs.

"Come with me," the first voice said.

Tom sighed. Someone was coming and on top of that had backup. He kept running, passing a nurse on the way. A few seconds later he heard the receptionist respond to a report about a possible intruder in the basement area. She asked the guards to check it out.

He ran into the cool room. It was empty, apart from a few wheeled stretchers used to cart bodies. The main wall was laid out like the boxes of a game TV show – door after door, each hiding a gruesome prize.

He had three locker numbers from bZane. He located the first one and pulled it open. The body was only a torso. He quickly closed it and went to the next one. It looked like her, or at least as close as he could tell. He checked the finger he had taken the sample from and to his surprise there was fresh healthy skin in its place. Part of her body had regenerated. She was definitely alive.

He doubted he'd be able to wheel her to safety in the little time he had. He pulled her out of the box onto one of the stretchers and covered her with a grey plastic sheet. He took the tag from her and swapped it for one in a nearby locker. He pushed the cart to the side of the room, creating a little hiding space for himself between the wall and the sheet hanging down the side of the cart.

Tom watched from his hiding space as the door opened and a man in an impeccable suit appeared with two goons following behind. They looked as if they were clones of Mr. Astin's bodyguards. PharmaCom were obviously chasing down any lead he happened to leave in his wake. The male nurse Tom had seen in the corridor above came after them.

"Why weren't the bodies identified?"

"Some of the bodies didn't have implants and they were so badly burnt it wasn't possible to id them in any other way. We are still following up with family for some of the people whose Omni- feeds were cut as a result of the explosion."

He opened three of the doors as he spoke, but found only two bodies.

"That's strange. There should be one more here."

"How about that one over there?"

Tom could only see the feet and ankles of the well-dressed man, but knew he was pointing his way. Tom pulled out the fibre Taser and waited. With a bit of luck he could take them all out.

"Let me check," the nurse said.

Tom could see his feet approaching, and swore to himself. He needed them all pretty close to each other to take them out at the same time. He doubted he'd get a second try once the bodyguards had seen him.

Tom held his breath as the nurse scanned the id tag. If he pulled the cover away even a little bit it would be all over.

"Ah, I see what's happened." The nurse opened the locker next to the empty one. "Someone must have put it in the wrong locker."

"She's not here," the well-dressed man said, frustration evident in his voice. "Let's go."

As they turned to leave, a guard opened the door from the outside. "We had a report of a possible grave robber. Have you seen anyone?"

"Seriously?" the male nurse frowned. "I made the report."

"Sorry, I'll check the rest of the area," said the guard, and left.

"Grave robber?" the well-dressed man asked.

"From time to time we get people trying to steal bodies."

"I see. We will see ourselves out."

"Take the elevator to the ground floor, turn left. Keep going and turn right. There are signs for reception."

The three men left the room.

The nurse moved the third body to the locker next to the other two bodies, then went to get the one Tom was hiding behind. Tom stood up when he was a few meters away.

"Who are you?" the nurse said, and took a step back.

"Sorry about this."

Tom pushed the trigger and a fine web of fibres attached to the nurse's upper body. A second later he convulsed as the electrical current surged through him. He fell where he stood, unconscious.

Tom immediately pushed the cart with the body out of the room and into the corridor. He didn't have long, minutes, maybe only seconds.

He tried to recall the layout of the morgue, but could only remember parts of it. The loading dock was at the back of the building, so he aimed in that general direction. He hailed a larger car to the location and immediately got a reject message. He shook his head. He hadn't considered he'd need special permission to hail a car to this location. He changed it to the front and received an acknowledgement.

He ran up the low incline ramp leading to the back of the building.

"At this location?" The well-dressed man's voice came through his earpiece. "We didn't see him here, but there was a report of an intruder."

Tom swore again. The nurse could wake up any second and now PharmaCom knew he was here too. He knew they'd still track him when they could, but he was surprised at how quickly they determined his location. He had been very careful in hiding his online tracks.

He pushed the cart through the door and looked around. The car he had ordered had an estimated arrival time of four minutes. It would be too late. He needed to get out of here now. Two transport vans stood parked at the other end of the parking lot. He pushed the cart towards them. It unlocked as he reached out his hand for the back door. Tom stopped for a second, but remembered the id tag he had loaded into his Omni. It was still active and the van must have read it as he approached.

He pushed Elize's body into the van and closed the back door. He heard the back door from the morgue open. Tom didn't even look back to see who it was. He jumped into the car and told it to drive to the nearest hospital. He watched the well-dressed man and his two goons in the side mirror. They would soon have a trace on the van and its destination. Tom swore. He couldn't really afford any more of bZane's help, but he didn't have a choice. He opened a two-way feed to the hacker.

"Devine, how did it go?" He paused for a few seconds. "Not very good, I can see. You've got a trace on the car you're in."

"Can you hide where I'm going?"

"I can make it look like you are still going to the Packer Memorial Hospital, sure, but it'll cost you."

"I'll pay."

"It won't keep them away for long. I was bored waiting for you to screw things up, so checked you out. They are tracking everything you do."

"Yeah, I know, but at the moment I just want to survive the next hour or two."

"At least change the id tag in your Omni."

"I have!"

"To a new one. They know about this one."

"Ok."

"You get this one for free. You don't have enough funds anyway. I checked your bank account. I'll do this one for you as a favour, but next time I expect full payment."

Tom loaded a new id tag in his Omni, sat back and directed the car to a new destination.

4

A Collaborator

Dr Tak ran one of the many clinics promising to stop the deterioration of the brain that the Drug caused in its later stages. Tom knew there was hardly any proof it helped; nevertheless, he had attended the clinic once a week for over a year. It focused on sensory-deprivation therapy, which, even if it didn't work, was the only time Tom felt he had full control over his wayward mind.

He had done a background check on Dr Tak before he started visiting the clinic. Until a few years ago, he had been a medical doctor, but official records just showed that he had stopped practicing. Tom's other channels showed a different story. He had caused the death of a number of deadheads as the result of experiments to cure them. This had been in the early days when the Drug was still legal and people still cared about what happened to deadheads, especially children of the wealthy.

Tom had helped him a few times with tracking down non-paying clients. He had no idea what to do with the body or even how to confirm whether it was alive or not. He hoped Dr Tak could help him.

Tom opened an encrypted, voice-only feed and selected Dr Tak's private Id tag.

"I didn't think we had any outstanding business," Dr Tak said, clearly irritated. Tom was one poorly chosen answer away from being disconnected.

"I need your help."

"In the middle of the night?"

"Yes."

"Go on."

"I have the body of Elize, the second posthuman."

"The body?" He was interested now. "She's dead?"

"I don't know. I can't tell."

"Wait."

The feed went quiet. It was possible Dr Tak would sell him out, but he had to take that chance. There was no one else he knew who could help, and he knew Dr Tak was still interested in the Drug and how to cure it.

"Take it to this address," Dr Tak said, and gave an address on the northern outskirts of the city.

Tom told the drive computer to alert him as soon as manual driving was permitted and assigned a destination many kilometres away from the address he was given. He sat back and watched as the night city landscape unfolded in front of him. It was the first time he felt he could relax enough to take stock of the situation. He had been acting on impulse ever since the explosion and now he knew he'd be a hunted man. Someone would soon put together the pieces and it would be an all-out manhunt. The only possible way he could survive it was to go completely off-grid, but he didn't want to do that. It didn't take a lot of self-examination to determine the cause of the impulses. This was his last opportunity to be part of something bigger, something that mattered. Adrian and Elize represented the future of humankind. They needed to be free to create a new world from the ashes of this one. If he could be a small part of making that happen before he faded away, his life would have had meaning.

"Manual control allowed," the drive computer advised. "Please be aware manual driving is the cause of 95% of all traffic accidents. Drive carefully."

Tom switched over. He knew this wouldn't help much. The car was still tracked by the network, but at least he didn't have to give a location to the drive computer. He stopped a few blocks away, unloaded the body and instructed the car to follow the highway that circled the city and make stops every few kilometres.

He carried the body to the destination. At first he thought he had come to the wrong address. A gap between two houses opened onto a small children's playground. It was one of those flukes of house numbering where a playground replaced a house, which meant it had its own street address.

A single streetlight created a cone of light in the centre of the playground, with everything else dimming into darkness. A young man was sitting on one of the swings, motionless. Like most people under 25, he had a completely integrated Omni, and it was obvious he was doing something with it. From the occasional twitches in his fingers, Tom guessed he was playing a game. Tom approached him slowly, wondering if he'd come to the right place. As he got closer, he no longer had any doubts. The boy was of Asian descent and the spitting image of his father. He wore baggy pants and a black hoodie with a swirl pattern on the front – expensive clothes designed to imitate what actual street kids wore. Tom hated the pretence.

As the more integrated systems almost completely disconnected you from what was going on around you, the Omni allowed greetings that interrupted the current activity. Tom never had much time for such niceties. He walked up to the pretend gangster and tapped him on the forehead. The young man jolted backwards, tangled up in the swing and fell in a heap.

His eyes regained focus as he disconnected from the game. He stared at Tom.

"Don't do that! Never heard of greets?"

"Never saw the point," Tom said with a grin. "Where's your dad?"

The young man reached out his hand and Tom helped him off the ground.

"Is that her?" he asked, ogling the wrapped body as he readjusted his clothing.

"It's Elize, yes. Where's your dad?"

"I'm TikTak," the young man said and held out his hand. An accompanying ping from Tom's Omni told him he had just received a feed greeting.

Tom frowned. He had noticed how young people nowadays used their feed ids instead of their real names even when off line.

"Cute," Tom said. "I'm Rainbow Shitting Unicorn. Now where's your dad?"

"I'll get our ride now," he said, and tuned out for a few seconds. "It is on its way."

TikTak kept staring at the body, but Tom ignored any of his attempts to strike up a conversation. He saw no reason to give away more than he had to, especially not to a kid he'd never see again.

A car drove up. It was one of the generic electric City Cars you rented by the hour.

"Don't worry," TikTak said. "I'll pay through an anonymizer payment gateway."

Tom shrugged. It wouldn't make much of a difference to the people who would be after him soon, but it bought time. TikTak helped put the body into the backseat and then set the end destination.

"Be seeing you, Rainbow Shitting Unicorn," TikTak said, and closed the car door.

The City Car drove back into the city and made a few stops before he came to familiar surroundings. The last stop was at the back of Dr Tak's clinic, where the doctor himself was waiting. He was pacing back and forth.

"How long do we have?" Dr Tak asked as soon as Tom opened the car door.

Tom appreciated his question. It meant he knew what was at stake.

"I'd say a couple of days, not more."

"Better get on with it then."

A few minutes later, Elize's body lay on a hospital bed. Dr Tak immediately began his investigation.

"Did you say she was in the centre of the explosion?"

Tom nodded.

"That is not consistent with her injuries. If she'd been in an explosion of the kind reported on the feed, all we'd need is a bucket and mop. These injuries aren't from heat. It looks more like acid burns. I can't say whether she has any internal injuries. I don't really have the equipment for it. Let's see."

He traced his hands over her body, stopping here and there to investigate further.

"A few broken bones, but that's about it. She's even missing a finger, but a blast that size would have literally torn her to pieces. I can't see anything to suggest she was anywhere near the explosion, so is there something you're not telling me?"

"That is all I know. This is what she looked like when I saw here there. Is she alive?"

"Yes, of sorts. She's in suspended animation."

Tom frowned. He had heard about breakthroughs in this area, but it still required a medical team to perform.

"Her blood has turned into ... something else. I will need to run tests to determine what it is, but my guess is her body has entered it as a response to severe shock. Whatever happened in there wasn't an explosion."

"I was there. It was an explosion."

Dr Tak stood back and watched the body.

"What about the brain?" Tom asked.

"It has shut down completely."

"So what now?"

"What do you mean?"

"What do we do with it?"

"Haven't you heard a word I've said?"

"Her brain has shut down. Her body is in suspended animation. I heard, but what do we do with the body?"

"We fix it," Dr Tak said.

This wasn't the person Tom had come to know. Dr Tak had been re-strained and formal. Now he was energetic, stimulated by the mystery. Tom liked this person much better.

"Her body turned off because of the shock of whatever happened to her in that explosion," he continued. "If we treat her injuries, my guess is she'll ..."

"Turn back on?" Tom said.

"Isn't she beautiful?" Dr Tak said suddenly.

Tom looked at the burned body and then at Dr Tak. He had never thought of her as beautiful, toasted or otherwise. She had been quite plain-looking.

"Her body has created new defence mechanisms," Dr Tak contin-ued. "She is a beautiful mystery."

"If you say so," Tom said finally. "Can you help her?"

"Of course I will help her. She will get the best care I can give her."

Dr Tak started immediately, doing a more thorough examination and starting to patch up the body. Tom watched for about ten minutes, but soon felt weariness creep over him.

"Thanks," Tom said and yawned. "I owe you."

Dr Tak just waved his hand dismissively.

"I will let you know how things are going via my son. It's better we don't meet again, I think."

Tom left the clinic and headed for home. He didn't know if he'd done the right thing, but he didn't really have many choices. He didn't know anyone else with any real medical experience. And he trusted Dr Tak, or at least he found him more trustworthy than most other peo-ple he knew. It would have to do, even if Tom knew this was only a very temporary solution.

He passed out on top of the bed fully clothed.

5

Escape

11:02am: Omni alerted of an incoming private feed.

11:15am: It alerted again.

11:22am: Tom woke up and rejected whoever was trying to reach him. He fell asleep, damning himself for not blocking it completely. Whatever it was could wait another hour or two.

Tom finally decided that the day began at 11:53am and had a breakfast of an approximation of coffee and a Vegemite sandwich. He wished he had real coffee, but hadn't been able to afford it since the introduction of the resource tax. Water-efficient alternatives had become the norm once the true cost of water was calculated into the price of everyday items.

Today he had a plan. He was ahead of everyone else, but it was unlikely to last long. If they even suspected he had Elize's body, they'd be coming with guns blazing. He had known there would be no going back from this as soon as he withheld information from Mr Astin – there were no second chances with people like him. The only way to stay alive was to stay ahead, and make sure you had something to bargain with when they caught up with you. His next step had to be to track down Adrian, or at least find out who had him. That information by itself was likely to keep him alive in the short term. The only solid lead he had was the apartment in the dead zone, so it was his first destination.

Thirty minutes later he sat on a train, his head surprisingly clear. It was as if having a purpose enabled his brain to function better. It made sense – focus allowed his frizzled-out brain to divert all its faculties to this singular task.

He pulled out his Omni and did a cursory check of the apartments across the street from his target. He wasn't too worried about finding something suitable. It was a dead zone, after all. When he arrived at his destination, he had four possible alternatives based on registered deadheads who were still signed on as owners of apartments.

He entered the block and knocked on the door of the first apartment. According to the registration details, a Lars Sorensen in his mid-fifties was the only occupant. He knocked again, analysing the lock as he waited. It was a proximity lock with fingerprint reader. It would only unlock if the lock knew your Omni and fingerprint pair. He didn't have anything to hack it quickly, even knowing they always had overrides that could be exploited. He knocked again and was just about to leave when the door opened, security chain still in place.

"Food distribution?" a female voice asked, her face only partially visible through the gap. She was young, no more than sixteen, he guessed.

"No, apartment audit," Tom said and flashed a long since expired police identity card. "According to our records a Lars Sorensen lives here. Who are you?"

Tom knew exactly who she was. She was a squatter. She'd moved in with Lars and ate most of his government-funded food. She'd make sure to be out of there during the infrequent visits from his family who'd be wondering why he was so slim, but probably secretly hoped he'd die and let them get on with life.

"I'm his daughter Evelyn," she replied immediately. "I'm just here visiting."

Tom made a show of checking his Omni and then nodded.

"Everything seems to be in order. Thank you."

She closed the door and he headed off for the next candidate. This time there was no reply. He was lucky. It was an old-fashioned lock, without any secondary identification. A self-configuring smart key would be enough to gain entry.

Less than five seconds later it had analysed the lock and moulded itself to the required shape. He turned the smart key, opened the door and stepped in. It was a three-bedroom apartment and it took him a little while to find the only occupant, a thirty-something woman who had crawled under a bed and was lying there in foetal position. She didn't acknowledge him so he closed the bedroom door.

The kitchen had a window facing the apartment block across the street. He pushed the kitchen table flush against the wall with the window and settled in. He knew he had a long wait. It might be days before anything happened. It didn't matter. There was plenty to do in the meantime. He pulled out his Omni and started checking the video cameras in the neighbourhood that he could access. A few were public and some had only minor security, which was easily hacked by software Tom had kept when he left the police force. To his surprise, none of the feeds was directed towards the apartment block. As he studied the video feeds from the cameras, he became convinced they had been moved or reprogrammed. It was just a bit too convenient that they all stopped just short of the door and the street outside. Apart from the frustration of having to set up his own camera, that didn't tell him much. Any organisation, government or private, could easily get that done, especially in a dead zone. He pulled out a small disposable video camera and set it up to take a continuous feed, two images a second.

Further research uncovered little. Most of the apartments in the building were government-owned, which wasn't surprising. Ten were privately owned and two were owned by small companies. This lead to the uncomfortable conclusion that he was more than likely up against some kind of government agency.

***

By evening, he had nothing but suspicions. Food administration employees had come and gone, which didn't confirm anything. He was just about to pack it in for the night when there was a knock on the door.

"Rainbow Shitting Unicorn, I know you are in there."

Tom opened the door, surprised to see TikTak standing there.

"How did you find me?"

TikTak ignored his question and stepped into the room, making sure to close the door and lock it.

"I have a message from my father. He says she is very much alive again, but there are no higher brain functions at this point."

The words came out too fast, as if the statement was just a formality before the real business began.

"That's great news. You tracked me down to tell me that?"

"No. I can't reach him any longer. He went offline over an hour ago."

"That's not necessarily ..."

"He never goes offline. Ever. I don't even think he knows how. Something's happened."

He had hoped for a few more days before they discovered Elize, but he had obviously been wrong. Dr Tak may just have something wrong with his connection, but it was unlikely. No one went offline any longer. The hassle it caused wasn't worth it. Tom couldn't afford to ignore this. Elize was his trump card. If he lost her he wouldn't survive beyond a few days. He needed something more. Tom packed his equipment and headed for the door.

"Are we going to get my father?"

"*We* are not doing anything," Tom said as he was running down the stairs with TikTak in hot pursuit. "How did you find me, by the way?"

"I put a tracker on you when we met yesterday."

"A tracker?"

"Yeah. I just added to the collection. You've got at least five more on you."

Tom nodded. He hadn't even considered trackers. It was so easy to track people through other means that putting a physical tag on someone just wasn't worth the effort. It appeared all his attempts trying to cover his tracks had earned him the dubious honour of getting special treatment.

"We need to get to my father's clinic," TikTak insisted.

"You do that," Tom said, as he hurried across the street. "I've got other things to do."

He didn't want to be too harsh with the boy, but at the same time he *did* have more important things to do and the last thing he wanted was a tagalong. He tried to work through the options for what could have happened to Dr Tak and Elize's body, but his brain again came up wanting. If he'd been on the Drug, he would just have formulated the question in his mind, which would generate a map of all relevant alternatives and the likelihood that they'd occur. As it was now, it would have to wait.

He tried the door to the building – it was open. He ran up three sets of stairs and down the hall. He'd already determined the number of steps needed to reach the apartment he had discovered the night before. As he got closer he could translate it to an actual apartment number. According to the register, one of the smaller companies owned it. He smiled. At least it wasn't a government operation.

He stopped at the door for a second as the realization of what he was about to do hit home. If this really was some kind of safe house for corporate operatives and he was discovered, he'd be dead as soon as they'd extracted whatever information they thought they could get from him. He knew this and still reached out to try the door. There was only a handle, the lock mechanism hidden in the door and frame. As he touched it, he could feel a slight vibration, which surprised him. It unlocked when he touched it. His own apartment door worked the same way – it read his bio identity from his hand and unlocked if programmed to do so. Why had this door been programmed to let him in?

He stepped into the dark hallway, closing the door behind him. From the outlines of the furniture it looked like just your average overnight apartment. He checked the two bedrooms. The apartment was empty. There were some clothes in one of the wardrobes, and after a more thorough search he found a small envelope pushed to the back of one of the bedside drawers. At first he didn't see anything in it, but sticky-taped to the inside was a small memTag. He placed it close to his Omni to allow access to its content, again ensuring it was not connected to the Omniscient Network. He selected the first item, an audio only media clip.

"I am God," it began. "I am the Devil. I am all-encompassing."

Tom stopped the playback of the audio clip and smiled. He couldn't believe his luck. The memTag was full of clips with Adrian's unmistakable, frantic, million-miles-an-hour verbal onslaught. He listened for a few more seconds. It sounded like a confession or maybe a diary. Whatever its purpose, Tom was sure there would be something in there he could use to find Adrian. Now all he needed was time to review it.

He changed his clothes for the ones in the wardrobe, hoping he didn't just swap one set of trackers for another. They fit surprisingly well. Even more surprising was that one of the pockets contained an id tag and a small amount of money. As he counted the money, the pieces finally began fitting together. This was one of Adrian's own safe houses. The people he had mistaken for operatives had been in his employ. The clothes he was wearing were there for the very reason he was wearing them now. This was a way for Adrian to swap identities quickly. He knew Adrian and Elize were almost impossible to track online. It wasn't so much that they weren't visible online, but their activity was equal to hundreds of people, making it impossible for automated agents to create coherency in their behaviour. Anyone actually wanting to know the whereabouts of either of them had to rely on CCTV footage and facial recognition, which was unreliable at best. There was even a small kit in his pocket designed to fool facial recognition software. That was why old-fashioned private investigators like Tom had been contracted in the first place. It was easier to follow them than try to make sense of their online tracks.

Someone knocked on the door and yelled, "This is the police. Open the door!"

At the exact same time, his Omni beeped. Someone was trying to reach him, which was impossible. His Omni was offline and he had loaded a completely new id tag in it. He checked it again. It was still of-fline, but the incoming message was there nonetheless.

Throw your clothes to the balcony below

He had no time to ponder the message. He didn't for a second be-lieve the people outside the door were the police, so whoever was send-ing the message was the best bet. He ran to the window and pulled it open.

"Open the door now!"

The door received another pounding.

He threw the clothes down to the small balcony below and the pounding stopped immediately.

"He jumped!" he heard a voice from the other side of the door and then the sounds of people running down the hall.

leave now

run

left to red door on right

enter

He knew he only had seconds to get out of there, so he followed the instructions. The door opened to the fire stairs. He started down, but was interrupted by another message.

up!

He ran. As he reached the top, he could hear footsteps further down. He wouldn't have long. He opened the roof access door and was re-warded with another message.

north

jump

Tom looked in the direction indicated. The building was slightly lower, but separated by an alleyway. It wasn't so much the distance as the idea of falling to a certain death that stopped him in his tracks. In other directions there were easier escape routes. Why had his mysterious helper suggested the most difficult option?

NOW!

Tom ran. If he timed the jump wrong he'd be dead, but at the same time, if he remained, he'd be dead too. He jumped. The Omni beeped in mid-air, alerting him to yet another message. He landed heavily and looked at his Omni.

Duck! Hide! Now!

He threw himself down, flushed up against the low wall that surrounded the roof. Soon he could hear voices on the other side.

"Scan the roof! I'm sure I saw him."

"Negative. There's no one here."

"Check nearby roofs."

Tom held his breath as he heard footsteps approaching. There was a gulf between him and his pursuers, but still so close.

"What do you think? Want me to check it?"

"There are easier escape routes. He wouldn't have chosen this one."

Tom smiled. Whoever was helping him had anticipated his pursuer's every move and even how they'd judge his flight. It smelled of someone amped up. A few minutes later he heard one of his pursuers give a status report.

"We've lost him. He might still be somewhere up on the roofs, so send in Rotors to scan the neighbourhood. We'll check the apartments one by one."

Tom heard the door close and immediately jumped to his feet. He had to get off the roof. The Rotor scan would pick him up immediately. He ran for the door leading off the roof and to his surprise found it open. Inside sat TikTak patiently waiting for him to appear.

"Can we go to my father's clinic now?"

"You did this?"

TikTak just smiled and headed down the stairs.

"We're on the same side, but we need to hurry."

"What side is that exactly?" Tom said, and shook his head.

"The side of the posthumans."

Tom followed silently. That was indeed his side, but he wondered how many sides this particular side had.

"How did you do it?"

"A magician never reveals his tricks."

Tom knew how to do it, but it would have taken him a day to prepare something like that. TikTak had done it in less than thirty minutes. It was just too much of a coincidence.

"You're not Dr Tak's son, are you?"

"This is not the time," he said, descending the stairs three steps at a time, "but yes, I am."

"I don't believe you?"

"No more talking. We need to hurry."

They ran down the last few flights of stairs and reached the ground floor.

"We can't go outside," Tom said. "The Rotor scan will pick us up."

"Don't worry. We've got another thirty seconds. As long as you keep your Omni disconnected, we'll be ok."

TikTak ran out the back door. A car was waiting on the street outside and he jumped in, Tom hot on his heels. It drove off at a leisurely pace, a complete anticlimax to the chase. Tom wanted to yell at TikTak to have him speed up, but he knew it was the right thing. Any behaviour out of the ordinary would immediately be picked up and investigated. Instead, he settled in and loaded the first of the many sound clips he had found in the apartment and sat back to listen.

6

Adrian's Audio Clip #1

I am God. I am the Devil. I am all-encompassing. Remember that and these recordings may make more sense to you.

However, I didn't start out that way. Once I was just like you, trying not to drown in the mediocrity of everyday life. I was paralysed by the endless options and always choosing whatever kept the status quo. You are such creatures of habit and I was one of you.

IntelEz changed all that when it was introduced in the market. Not just for me, but for everyone else too. I didn't try it at first, would you believe? I thought it must have serious side effects, but after a year of use, people around me still seemed ok so I tried it. It was the most exhilarating experience I'd ever felt. To start with, I just felt the information flow over me and watched as different, unrelated pieces of experience, memory, emotions and senses connected into a tapestry of unbelievable beauty. Every move I made, every new fact I added, sent a ripple through its fabric, constantly rearranging it.

At first, I just stared at the inter-connectedness. I traced the decision tree, discovering there was an 11 percent risk of dying if I climbed down the face of the building. I studied it further and found this figure had been determined based on the layout of the facade, my physical characteristics, the weather and many more factors. I knew all this information was available to me through different means. I had seen the outside of the building often enough. I had read a weather report and I had been outside just minutes earlier. I knew my general physical state and what I was capable of, but this was only the beginning. I could easily trace these facts to recent history. Added to this was information about architecture, strength of materials, wind patterns and more. My mind was able to access most, if not all, the information I had been exposed to throughout my life and use this to assess actions and their outcomes. I had never been aware that it could be used, nor would I ever have attempted to calculate this nonsensical figure.

And yes, I did climb down the face of the building that very moment. It was the most exhilarating thing I had ever done. I pitted my life against a number for no other reason than I could. I stepped from a world with endless worries about the most trivial decisions, to one where hard numbers informed every action I took.

It redefined me in ways I don't have the time or language to describe. I now understood why people all over the world were using it. This was how life was meant to be lived. Everything began making sense, and with understanding, surprisingly, came caring. I had never cared about much apart from myself. Now I could see the ripple effect on the world as I navigated through it. Even peripheral people in my life were of interest. It was exhilarating, even arousing, to introduce a new person into the tapestry of my life and see all the possible ways they could affect it.

The world around me was changing too. As more and more people were using the Drug, a greater understanding between nations developed. We each live in our own little world, with ignorance making us look only to ourselves. But we are all connected in so many ways. The most appropriate use of resources is possible only when everyone involved in the negotiations can see it from a bigger perspective than maximizing their own benefit. Science followed suit. The Drug triggered new developments in all scientific fields. A golden age had begun and I was riding its wave.

As my interest in life expanded, I also found a greater fascination in smaller things and in perfecting every aspect of my life. I designed the perfect cup of coffee with the local barista. I refined equations to describe a more effective way of walking. There seemed to be an endless list of things to improve, starting with the small and working my way up.

On the way up, I turned to women and sex. Before my change, I was very basic in what I looked for. I preferred blonde, petite women, who weren't so smart they could show me up, but not so dumb they annoyed me – as I said, pretty basic – but that didn't keep me from failing with most women I pursued. Now I could have my pick. I didn't consider it then, but for some reason I was able to find the one thing that would stimulate her mind whether she was on the Drug or not.

The Drug had changed my preferences. It was no longer just a question of sexual attraction and the lowest possible annoyance factor. Beauty was found as much in function as in form. And what an amazing function woman is. A design allowing not only the creation of life, but also the nurture of it. In comparison, man is simply primal instincts thrown together in a chest-beating mess. It was almost embarrassing to make the comparison. My preference now was for curvy women with childbearing hips, strong but still delicate.

My admiration of women didn't stop there, of course. Like many others who find themselves suddenly popular, I engaged in sex as often as I could, and found I could enhance the feelings tenfold by feeding all my senses on the experience. The angle of the hip as it thrust became an equation. Any sexual act I could imagine – they all became formulas I could repeat in my mind. Soon I didn't need anyone else. I could recycle the equations in my head and build up an orgasm greater than I could ever reach with the imperfection of a partner. I spent days and nights perfecting those formulas and then days and nights test-driving them until fatigue eventually stopped me. It may sound strange, but this cured me of one of my primal instincts. Sex no longer held any interest for me. Perhaps I had burnt out the ability to feel anything from it, or maybe it was the realization that I had calculated perfection. In any case, I had reached the end and there was nothing beyond to tantalize the senses. That, I'm afraid, is perfection. Once you've reached it, you no longer want it.

You may wonder why I tell you this, but bear with me. I didn't realize it then, but I had stumbled on something of enormous importance.

Something that will redefine humankind. Something that could redefine you.

7

Body Hunt

Streetlights aligned with the few stars that could be seen through the ever-present clouds. Together with reflections from windows and puddles on the road, they sent Tom's brain into a tailspin trying to find a pattern. The only thing the conscious Tom could think before disappearing in a torrent of numbers, equations and pattern analysis was, "Not again!"

Tom no longer had an identity. The elusiveness of the pattern required all his mental faculties. He had become the pattern recognition process. For however long it would take, solving the riddle was his sole purpose in life. But Tom had no say in it. He wasn't even consciously aware of what he was doing.

***

"Finally," TikTak said, as Tom sat up and buried his head in his hands. "Take this," he said, and held out a small pill and a bottle of eWater. "I have a friend who is close to the end too. She finds these help."

Tom didn't ask what it was. He wanted to curl up in a little ball and force himself to tune out and eventually fall asleep. His whole body felt drained, as if his blood no longer could be bothered to sustain it. He could have sworn his brain was a couple of sizes too big for his skull. He resisted the urge to hold his ears to stop it from draining out through his ear canals.

"How long?" Tom asked.

"I don't know. An hour. Perhaps a bit more."

Tom swallowed the pill and drank the whole bottle of eWater. To his surprise, he felt better after only a few minutes. There was no denying his episodes were getting worse. Tom tried to remember the charts showing the deterioration based on frequency and length – six months, twelve if he was lucky.

TikTak stepped out of the car and stood watching his father's clinic. Tom knew he was running checks. There was no doubt TikTak was some kind of operative, but where was his real allegiance?

"Let's go," Tom said, and joined TikTak on the sidewalk.

"Are you sure? I've done a scan of the building and it looks clean, but the clinic itself is off the grid. I can't see anything in there. I've asked for backup, but I don't know when they'll arrive."

"We don't have time. Let's go," he repeated, and pulled the Taser from his inside pocket.

"Nice," TikTak said with a grin. "Never took you for a humanitarian."

"I'm pretty sure if I hold down the trigger long enough someone will die."

"Just don't use it anywhere near me," he said, pulling out a metal handle and extended it to a rod with a flick of his wrist. "It's a bit too indiscriminate for my liking."

"So what does that do?" Tom eyed the rod suspiciously. It was thin rod, about 50 centimetres long, with a small sphere at the end and it looked as low-tech as you could possibly get.

"It is a tactical baton. You beat people over the head with it and they fall down," TikTak said, and handed him a small flashlight and a pair of goggles. "You may need these. I've checked what I can. I'm sure there is some kind of surveillance here, but I've not been able to detect any. Once we enter, I don't think we'll have more than five minutes, so we have to work fast. We want to secure the body or someone who might know where it is."

"Sounds good to me," Tom said, as he checked that the flashlight and goggles were set to the same frequency. They were light spectrum aligned, allowing him to see whatever the light from the flashlight illuminated without anyone else seeing it. "Let's go."

The door to the clinic was closed, but TikTak purposefully strode up and pulled it open, with a certainty that could only come from knowing it wasn't locked. It was pitch black inside. Tom knew the layout of the clinic and was sure TikTak would know it too. The door opened into a reception area, which had nice couches along the walls for the waiting patients. A corridor straight ahead led to the treatment rooms.

TikTak entered first and was immediately swallowed by the darkness within. Tom put on the goggles and switched on the flashlight. He could see TikTak making his way towards the corridor. He followed and closed the door behind him. He immediately sensed that something was wrong. They weren't alone in here. His tired mind couldn't pinpoint exactly what was raising the alarm, but he knew better than to doubt his instincts. He swept the flashlight over the reception area, but couldn't see anyone. He turned back to the corridor and realised with alarm that TikTak was no longer there.

He saw something move in the corner of his eye, but when he turned towards it, there was nothing there. This repeated over and over, until he took a few steps forward and froze as he felt something against the back of his head.

"Drop the ... whatever it is," a voice hissed behind him.

It seemed impossible that someone could have hidden anywhere in the room, but whoever it was had made a mistake. Tom might not be able to see him, but he knew where he was. He swivelled around, knocked the assailants arm aside and pushed the button on the Taser. The electrical discharge fizzled in the air. A gagging sound came from the nothingness in front of him. He held the button until there was a loud thud. He kept holding the button until there was no more movement.

"Shit!" The voice had come from behind him.

Tom turned around and saw motion, but nothing else. A strike towards the side of his head threw him into the wall. He lost his grip on the flashlight and Taser as he struggled to stay conscious.

The clinic was suddenly flooded with light. Tom pulled off the goggles and stared up at the three shapes in front of him.

"He's tough," a voice marked with a permanent sneer said.

"I wish people would stop doing that," Tom said as he touched the side of his head just behind the ear. It was already swelling up. He wondered how much more damage his head could take before it just gave up and caved in.

"I think Zemer is dead," a female voice said.

"Tasered to death? What a way to go. Do you think you'd black out or stay conscious for it?"

"I told you not to underestimate him."

Tom sat up and tried to focus. He wanted to confirm what he already knew – that the last comment had been from TikTak.

"I read his report," the sneering voice said. "He's known to not carry weapons, so where did that come from?"

Tom could finally put a face to the voice. Everything but his skin colour was black – short cut black hair and eyes that seemed to be all pupil. He wore black combat gear and held a rod similar to the one TikTak had. Tom didn't doubt he was in charge. His posture, everything about him said authority. The woman next to him was tall and blond with blue eyes. She was dressed the same as the man, making her look like a GI Barbie.

"I hate technology," Tom said, pulling the goggles off his head. "I couldn't see you because of these stupid glasses."

"This is the backup," TikTak said with an apologetic shrug. "Marksman, Ellen and Zemer. We're part of EvoII."

Tom had heard about them. He had dismissed them as an extremist macro-evolution organisation, the militant version of a posthuman interest group.

"We need to get out of here," Marksman said, "I'm pretty sure his little plaything can be tracked. Someone's cleaned this place already, anyway."

"Perimeter zone has been breached," TikTak said. "I think we already have company."

"We'll give them something to chase," Marksman said with a grin. "You get out unseen if you can. We'll meet back at the centre."

Marksman and Ellen ran out the door, leaving TikTak and Tom.

"Are you OK to walk?" TikTak said. "We need to get out of here."

"I'm fine, I've had worse. Just yesterday, in fact. What makes you think I'm coming with you though?"

"I will explain everything, but we're dead if we stay here any longer."

"I'm dead anyway," he said, and shrugged.

"There should be a back door down this way," TikTak said, and headed down the corridor.

The corridor turned and at the end was a fire exit. TikTak ran towards it, but was too late. The door opened, revealing a man in a dark suit. He held a small-calibre gun aimed at the floor. TikTak didn't stop. He ran a few more steps and threw himself forward, the black rod raised.

As the man in the doorway shifted his weight to take aim, Tom saw another man behind him. Tom steeled himself for a shot that never came. TikTak struck the gun so hard that the man's wrist broke, and followed up with a quick strike to the head, pushing him towards the second man and jumped as the first attacker fell. The second man took a step back, but TikTak just shifted his weight in the air, turning the landing into a cat roll. He shattered the man's knee with the rod as he got back to his feet. TikTak finished him off like the first.

Tom just stared. It had taken TikTak a few seconds to take out two armed opponents with what amounted to a fancy stick.

"We need to go now," TikTak said, as he looked for more attackers.

Tom did too, but this was the extent of it – for now.

"Follow me."

Tom obeyed. They ran down a block and turned into a small side street where the car was parked.

"What's going on?" Tom asked, as he jumped into the car.

"You know anything about EvoII?"

"I know the basics. You think Adrian and Elize are the next step in evolution and you want to be part of that."

"Yeah, that about sums it up," TikTak said. "We're a voluntary organisation sworn to protect and further the posthumans. We have many different sections. I'm part of research."

"Research?" Tom laughed, and then winced from the pain his laughter caused. "Looks like you forgot your lab coat for this mission."

"Research requires field missions that can't be left to knuckleheads like Marksman."

"Are you really Dr Tak's son? Because I don't buy it."

"I am. I've been with EvoII since it started about a year ago and I've been trying to recruit my father since then. When you contacted him, he contacted me in turn. To be honest, I didn't believe it, so I checked you out on my own. After we dropped the body off at the clinic, my father told me not to tell my friends at EvoII anything yet. I obeyed, but perhaps I shouldn't have. In the afternoon he contacted me, this time telling me that her body was alive, but that her brain was still very much dormant. He said he needed to move the body, and I volunteered that my friends and I could do it. Truth to be told, I had already told them about it. He agreed, so I set it up. He was going to take the body to one of our clinics this afternoon. That was the last I heard from him."

"Ok," Tom said. "So you went chasing me."

"I figured he'd contacted you directly."

"So someone's got him and Elize?"

"Seems like it."

"Where are we going?" Tom said, as he checked his surroundings.

"Back to our base. We'll be safe there for now."

"I'm going to rest. Wake me up when we get there."

The situation was spiralling out of control at an alarming rate. Tom had a few cards yet to play, but somehow it didn't matter. On his own he wouldn't last another day, so he had no choice but to align himself with a group. EvoII was a bad bet, but the only one that didn't mean immediate incarceration or death.

One of the cards he held was Adrian's diary. The last words he remembered promised something that could redefine humankind. He scanned the clip and found the place, sat back, closed his eyes and listened, hoping to find out what it was.

8

Adrian's Audio Clip #2

Context is everything. In this case, context is history. My rise to fame came from the realization I had reacted very differently to IntelEz from everyone else.

Would you believe it was one of those new game shows where people show off how smart they are that gave me a clue? Now that anyone could be a mental athlete, these shows became very popular. I had sixteen TV screens set to swap channels every ten seconds. I hardly ever watched them. It was enough to leave them on to take in the consumable version of what was going on in the world. A snippet of one of those TV shows played and I caught one of the contestants struggling with a math problem that was immediately obvious to me. I sat down and watched as all the contestants answered questions and mulled over problems that would have had a Nobel Prize winner struggling prior to the Drug. After watching a whole episode, I calculated I was at least three times more intelligent than the winner.

You probably know what happened. I entered the TV shows, won everything there was to win, and turned into the shiniest boy of the IntelEz golden age. Everyone wanted to be me. IntelEz use skyrocketed. I never had any messianic ambitions. I just wanted to try out being famous, just as I had been working on the perfect cup of coffee before that.

It wasn't long before I had my own TV show. I did stadium-sized events where I showed off how smart I was. I solved the six remaining Millennium Prize Problems in a series of these events and went on to decline the award, much as Grigori Perelman who solved the first one had. My efforts to become famous pushed the mass adoption of the Drug worldwide.

Ego doesn't disappear with intelligence. If anything, it gets bigger, and for good, calculable reasons. The smarter you are, the more valuable you are for the development of the species. I was able to quantify this; thus, I had an objective measure of my own worth. On the other side of the coin, you have the realisation that your ego can only thrive in the network of everyone else. Not just family and friends, and not just as a country, but also on a global scale.

As more and more turned to IntelEz, this became apparent. Global initiatives began. Finite resources all of a sudden became very expensive, forcing innovation in alternate approaches, recycling and renewable sources. A world virtual currency was proposed and accepted. Many in the financial sector found themselves without a job, as the accumulation of wealth for the few no longer was the prime objective. The complex rules and regulations were discarded to allow funds and resources where needed, based on a globally agreed action plan. However, you know all this. You lived through it, after all.

At that point, I had long since stopped taking IntelEz. My body was able to produce a natural equivalent. This was not something I set out to do. My body had probably always been able to do it and my first dose triggered it. I could also see that my decision tree was deepening. The average depth had changed from a few hours to days. The complexity had increased too. Every node in the tree now had an average of six choices, when before there had been three. Granularity had also expanded. My mind was processing the world in the same way a powerful computer processes all possible moves in a chess game, but where the computer had perfect knowledge of chess, the boundaries for the game completely known, I was dealing with a seemingly random world. No computer could do what I did now.

What do you do with that? I was already one of the most famous people in the world. I had made more money that I could possibly spend even if I tried. I had a number of companies generating even more money. I had no interest in any kind of leadership position. I had less and less interest in other people. Their on-rails existence was so predictable I could no longer even pretend to be interested. From what I could understand, I was a race of one. What can you possibly achieve when you are the only one of your kind?

I made plans. Childish, uninformed plans, and I will not bore you with the details. They were all interrupted by the golden age coming to an abrupt end. The first case rippled through the fabric of my future existence. A ten-year-old child, Victor Meme, had been on extraordinary high doses since he was six, administered by his loving parents. They had happily ignored the health warnings for developing brains, hoping he could become the next me. That was the reason they gave. Of course, the whole world turned on me, citing what a poor role model I was for children. I had never set out to be a role model for anyone, especially not children. They are an inefficient by-product of development, a must to further the species. I had some ideas on how to change that, but knew it was pointless to suggest them, especially now that I was children's enemy number one.

Victor developed severe autism, or at least a variant of it. His brain no longer had the ability to process the collected input from his senses, so he withdrew into a state which limited any new input. IntelEz opened the floodgates of information, but the process was irreversible. The mind was left to fend for itself, whether it could handle it or not.

Victor's case was dismissed as an obvious case of Drug misuse, but I knew it wouldn't end there. I cancelled all appearances and prepared for the coming storm.

More cases followed, invariably children in circumstances similar to Victor's. It wasn't long before adults who used large amounts of the Drug started reporting having blackouts.

The world slowly came to realize this was not an isolated occurrence. When the first fully fledged case of an adult turning autistic surfaced, everyone again turned to the poster boy of the Drug for explanations.

By then I had removed myself from the equation. I had taken on another identity – several, actually – and was moving between lodgings similar to the one where you found these files. The consensus was that I too was autistic, and possibly dead. This suited me fine. Fame no longer held any interest for me.

Soon the world had more important things to worry about than whether the smartest man on the planet was, in fact, alive. Local economies went into tailspins as a third of their workforce suddenly disappeared. The recently established world market collapsed in a heap, but again I am telling you what you already know. As soon as the first case had appeared, it was obvious there would be a collapse, so I changed my investment strategies accordingly. Once the crisis hit, I was, if anything, even richer.

There was no longer any claim on my time and I again began ruminating over the purpose of it all. I could trace actions and reactions over months, and focusing on a single thread, I could usually follow it to all possible end states. This I realised was being all knowing, just as the Christian God was purported to be. Sure, I worked with probabilities, where God didn't need to, but who cares? At some point the distinction is too small to make a difference.

Another realization that quickly followed was that being God was pointless. If you know or can calculate everything, what's the point? Is God sitting there with a checklist and just ticking things off as all the known states pass by? God in that context has no purpose, and I realised the same went for me. I was nothing more than a monkey, the smartest one perhaps, but still just a monkey, banging my digital rocks together. I needed a purpose. Something grand. Something befitting the God I'd become.

9

Evoll

TikTak studied the man next to him.

Tom was asleep or at least it looked that way – his face always seemed set in a frown. Now that he was relaxed, half lying down in the car seat, he looked so old. TikTak knew he was thirty-six, but he looked closer to fifty. His dark hair was turning grey. TikTak had seen photos of Tom in his mid-twenties. He'd been quite handsome, making it hard to imagine what could have happened. Now he looked like an ageing movie star that had let himself go.

The car had stopped maybe twenty minutes ago, but TikTak didn't have the heart to wake him up. Tom had had a rough ride the past couple of days, from what he could tell. He couldn't delay it much longer though. Lotti would want to meet the man who had become such a big part of the posthumans' last few days. He reached out to give Tom a shake and noticed the wired earplugs. TikTak shook his head. Nowadays, most people had them integrated into the inner ear or at least had semi-permanent inserts into the ear canal. He had even seen him use and old Omni with a touch screen. As he leant forward, he noticed there was even some sound leakage. Tom was listening to a voice recording.

TikTak was all of a sudden very interested in what it could be. He hadn't picked Tom for an audiobook kind of person. He gently took hold of the wire and pulled the earphone out of Tom's ear. He inserted it into his own ear, frowning at the uncomfortable experience. It took a few seconds for the earpiece to mould itself to his ear.

"What possible interest could life hold for me when all outcomes were known?" TikTak heard. "Sure, there were less likely paths that could potentially be taken, but they were all known states. I know this is not strictly true. There was an element of randomness I couldn't foresee and a potential shift in parameters that could have unexpected consequences. But in the same way as ants in enough numbers could be irritating …"

Tom suddenly moved and TikTak immediately removed the earpiece from his own ear, took hold of the wire and pulled the other one out of Tom's ear.

"Time to wake up," he said. "You've got places to go, people to meet."

"Yeah, ok," said Tom, as he sat up and looked around. "Where are we?"

TikTak had heard enough of the recording to know it was Adrian speaking. He had spent many hours watching the TV show that made Adrian famous to learn what he could about the posthuman. He couldn't work out why Tom would be listening to him apart from getting to know every aspect of his quarry. There was something that didn't feel right about that explanation, an immediate gut reaction he had learnt to trust, but in this case he had no idea what it meant. He didn't have time to worry about that now though.

"This is our main base," TikTak answered. "You'll be safe here."

"Safe? Yeah, right."

TikTak could hear the tired sarcasm in Tom's voice and it irritated him.

"You think you'd be better off with anyone else?" he snapped back.

"No," Tom said tentatively, and then added, "No, you're right. You've saved my life a couple of times already today. Thank you."

Tom stretched as he got out of the car.

"So where is this base of yours?"

TikTak nodded towards the building on front of them. They had taken over an old abandoned hotel, barred up the windows and made it into a fortress, the big glassed-in vestibule on the ground floor the only feature remaining.

"Marksman," Tom said. "How well do you know him?"

"I know him well enough," he answered, deciding not to go into detail about their past. "He was a mercenary before he joined. A bit on the extreme side, but gets things done."

That was the understatement of the century, but TikTak wasn't sure whether he trusted the private investigator. Marksman believed in the cause completely and totally. He'd sacrifice anyone, including himself, to reach EvoII's goal. He believed anarchy was the only way to pave the way for the future. TikTak disagreed. He even questioned whether the posthumans were a good idea. They seemed such a giant leap in development. Surely there would be a price to pay to leap into the future like that?

"Is his tag really Marksman? I mean, how did he get one of the originals? It isn't Marksman342 or something?"

"No, he's the genuine article. I don't know if he just got in at the right time, but I heard someone say he found the person who had the tag and made him give it up."

"He looks like a crazy fuck to me."

"That he is."

Three armed guards greeted them as they entered the building. TikTak didn't know them, but they obviously knew him. One of them nodded and stepped aside.

He had been asked to report directly to one of the meeting rooms on the second floor. They passed the reception area, through a corridor to the stairs. He hurried past a barricade halfway up the stairs and into the second-level corridor. This area had been the business centre in the hotel and had four meeting rooms connected to an octagonal reception hall.

They entered the first meeting room. TikTak was surprised to see all group leaders around the table. Something important must have happened for them all to gather at this time. Lotti, the leader of EvoII, was sitting at the head of the table. They all turned to the new entrants expectantly.

"We were not able to secure Elize's body. Secondary mission completed successfully."

"I'm …" Tom began.

"I know who you are," Lotti's eyes drilled into his. "Tom Leonard Devine. Mother and father dead. One child, deceased. Marriage to Indra Barton ended two years ago. Decorated detective. Thrown out of the police force for theft. The timing of these events makes it likely they are interconnected."

"Enough," Tom said, and looked down.

TikTak had seen Lotti do this many times. Everyone had something to hide and Lotti used it to gain advantage, a way to show dominance. If there was something she was good at, it was forcing her will on people. TikTak knew that from first-hand experience.

Tom swayed on his feet then looked up again, locking eyes with Lotti.

"Lotti Genzberg," Tom said. "Forty years old. Living under a completely fabricated identity. Born Marsha Lang in a small town she no longer wants to remember the name of. Greatest achievement was third place in a beauty pageant when she was seventeen. Has changed her name four times since. A fixture of any extremist organisation promising social upheaval. The timing of these events makes it likely they are interconnected."

TikTak just stared at Lotti, struggling to suppress a smile. He had no idea how Tom could possibly know these things, and yet from Lotti's expression they were obviously true. She looked like she had been hit in the face. All eyes were on Lotti to see how she'd react.

Marksman entered the room.

"There you are," he said, and then frowned as he saw the pissing contest taking place.

"You don't know anything," Lotti said finally, dismissing Tom with a wave of her hand. "Get rid of him."

"I know a thing or two," Tom said. "But I'll only discuss it with your leader. Surely you're not it?"

Marksman smiled like a predator watching his lunch struggle.

"If you've got anything, say it now," Lotti said.

"I need something to eat and some rest. After that, absolutely."

"You know nothing ..." Lotti began, but Tom interrupted her. "And to show my allegiance with your cause, I give you this."

He put a small vial on the table.

TikTak leant forward to get a better look, but was too far away to determine what it was.

"This is a tissue sample from Elize," Tom said, "I took it before handing the body over to Dr Tak."

Dr Menker, leader of the research section, snatched the vial from the table and studied it intently, as if hoping it would yield its secrets from a cursory examination. "I need to analyse this," he said, and left the room.

"So how about the food and rest?" Tom asked.

"We'll talk later," she said. Two junior members led Tom away.

"Full status report," she said, turning to Marksman.

"Not much to tell, unfortunately. Someone had been there before we came. No sign of a body or even that it had ever been there. The local servers did have memDrive slots, but the drives were either never installed or taken when the body was removed."

"Any idea who was behind it?"

"No. We had a run-in with some agents. Private ones, from the look of them. I'm guessing they were after the same as us."

"So we don't know who took the body?"

"No," Marksman said.

"Dr Tak still has the body," Emerus Lorre, the leader of the intelligence group, said. "I've found footage from a nearby cam. It shows Dr Tak leaving the clinic in a company car. I crosschecked with the driver network, but the navigation system must have been disabled."

"We can assume everyone else has this footage too, and possibly more. So where was he going?"

Everyone's eyes turned to TikTak.

"I can only think he's either contacted another group or some old contact. I'll put together a list of candidates, but it won't be complete."

"Give me what you can," Lotti said. "We can run it through a Social Analyser. Should add a few more names hopefully."

"So what do we do with the private detective?" Marksman said. "I think he's bluffing. I say get rid of him."

"I'm inclined to agree," Lotti said.

No one around the table objected. There were even a few nods.

TikTak couldn't believe what he was hearing. "I think that would be a mistake," he said carefully. "We've got nothing to go on for either of the posthumans. I believe Tom has had contact with both of them in the past 48 hours. He could still be useful."

"How do you figure that?

"I think the apartment where I picked him up was connected to Adrian somehow."

"Based on what?"

"His behaviour. To my knowledge he only has one contract and he was prepared to watch the apartment for days. I think he is one step ahead of all of us."

As he said it, a piece in the puzzle suddenly clicked into place in his mind. Tom had indeed found something in that apartment. The recording Tom had been listening to in the car had come from there. He was just about to tell them when he thought better of it. It was a very political environment in the group now. He needed to work out how he could use the information to his advantage.

"Find out what he knows," Lotti said. "Then we'll get rid of him."

TikTak nodded.

"You can go," she said.

TikTak and Marksman left the room.

"How many?" Marksman asked as they walked down the corridor.

"Two in the hospital."

Marksman nodded.

"One in the hospital and one in the morgue," Marksman said, "I win."

"Even. Killing doesn't increase the score. If anything it should be worth less. Disabling takes more skill than killing."

"Where's the fun in that?" Marksman said with a grin. "Do you know what the meeting's about?"

TikTak shook his head.

"You used to know everything that was going on. I take it you and Lotti no longer ..."

"No, we're not."

"A shame."

"A shame? Why?"

"It could have been useful, that's all."

TikTak didn't like what he was hearing. He knew there was no love lost between Lotti and Marksman. They had such diametrically opposed viewpoints that they always argued about every little detail. He hadn't liked her at first either, but had soon succumbed to her will. When she wanted something, she went after it to a point where it was either hers or was no longer relevant. He had seen both happen.

"There are many of us who think she's not taking this organisation in the right direction, and the detective's stunt in there just helped convince us."

"Count me in," TikTak said.

Marksman only nodded and went on his way. TikTak wasn't sure what to do. He had no intention of aligning himself with Marksman and his crowd, but he knew which way the wind was blowing. Lotti, for all her posturing, was on her way out and he was in her camp. He was sure he was safe as long as Elize's body was missing and Tom still had secrets to spill, but that wouldn't hold for very long. He could just leave, but he knew Marksman would come after him. Marksman didn't like loose ends.

He realised then that Marksman hadn't asked him about the meeting to find out its reason. He already knew. He just wanted to find out if TikTak had known. Therefore, it must have been about the leadership.

TikTak hated what the organisation had become. He had joined because he believed humankind faced a choice of either imploding or changing into something else entirely – or perhaps both. IntelEz had seemed to be the answer and in a way it was. It had showed humankind what it could be – and then pulled the rug out from under its feet. The posthumans were the extension of the hope that IntelEz had provided.

When he joined, EvoII was furthering the posthumans any way possible. Lotti had been the driving force behind this stance and no one questioned it. He had questioned her motives at the time, but overall it had worked towards a goal that all the members shared. This had changed when more people like Marksman had joined. The organisation had fractured into camps, still with a more or less shared goal, but with very different ideas of how to get there. He had never tried to align himself with any group and as a result had become part of Lotti's ever-diminishing supporters by default.

He realised he didn't know who he could trust anymore. Lotti, yes, but he couldn't see what she could do. Which led him to the only other person he believed he could trust – Tom.

TikTak knew where he'd be. There were a few smaller rooms on the level above. They were mainly used by interstate members needing somewhere to sleep for the night. They could also be locked from the outside. He took the stairs and found Tom in the third room he checked.

"What do you want?" Tom said. He was lying on the narrow sofa bed with his jacket over him as a blanket. There was a tray with a half-eaten meal on the table.

"We need to talk."

"In here?" Tom said with an amused smile.

TikTak knew why he asked. Tom expected the room was wired and he was correct.

"I want to find out what you know about Elize and where she is."

"Shouldn't you know? Your father ran off with her."

TikTak wrote a message on an old Omni he had brought along for this very purpose. He showed it to Tom: "I know about Adrian's recordings."

Adrian frowned, took the Omni and started writing. Two conversations began.

Tom: Clever boy. So what?

"Doesn't mean I know where he is," TikTak said, whilst typing furiously. "He's gone underground and we need to find him before anyone else does. You know we're a better bet than anyone else."

TikTak: Can we locate Adrian with them?

Tom: We?

TikTak: You and I.

"Yeah, there is that," Tom said after a while, as if he needed time to think about it. He was smiling as he wrote a reply.

Tom: No friends in EvoII any longer?

TikTak: Something like that.

"We have good medical facilities here," TikTak said, finding it difficult to keep track of the two conversations. "We can help her back. And you know we're on her side."

Tom: I'll think about it.

TikTak: Not much time.

"OK, OK, you've done your sell," Tom said. "I do have information, but I'm not sure how best to use it. If I could get my Omni back, I might be able to get my hands on it."

Tom: There never is.

"I'll get you your Omni back," TikTak said, and pocketed his own after reading Tom's final message.

"No hurry," Tom said and yawned. "The sleep of the just is calling."

"The sleep of the just barely," TikTak said under his breath, as he left the room. He didn't lock it. If they wanted Tom to be a prisoner, someone else could enforce it.

As he walked to his next destination, his mind kept coming back to Elize. She was an enigma, to say the least. Everyone knew about Adrian. He had been a regular fixture on the feed for over a year. His story was well known. Exactly how he'd become what he was, was still a mystery, but there were hours and hours of interview material where Adrian was discussing and providing theories for it. They had followed up on all of them, but none had proved successful.

Hardly anyone knew anything about Elize. She had not revealed her existence like Adrian, so if it hadn't been for the war they waged, no one would have known about her. There were no tests, no easy way to detect a posthuman, and it raised the question of other undisclosed posthumans. There was a group within EvoII focusing on exactly that. The western world focused on Adrian, but there was reason to believe there were others.

Perhaps the greatest mystery came from the fact that Adrian and Elize had known each other before they became posthumans. They had been married, in fact. The majority of the research community agreed that this pointed to some kind of environmental factor they had both been subjected to. Yet another group within EvoII was dissecting every known fact about Adrian and Elize and their life together, trying to learn what environmental factor might have contributed to the change.

On a whim, TikTak poked his head into the laboratory where Dr Menker was ordering his team around, trying to solve the riddle of the small sample he had been given.

"Found anything?" he asked.

Dr Menker didn't look away from the computer screens. "It is just as you said. Her body has somehow transformed the blood to allow for a short-term suspended animation. Like a freezing agent. We haven't even begun to work out how such a change is even possible. It would require organs we don't have and changes down on a cellular level. We always assumed the changes were mainly in the mind, but this ..." Dr Menker shook his head in wonder, "is a sample of a new species."

"Cellular changes?"

"There are pockets of stem cells throughout the sample able to re-generate new specialised cells, and the normal cells also have different characteristics. Most likely this is for self-healing. We think she'd be able to regrow parts of her body or even battle cancer."

"That makes no sense," TikTak said, and was finally rewarded with Dr Menker's undivided attention.

"I know. IntelEz only affects your brain, so where do the physical changes come from? We are starting to think there might a primary physical mutation occurring before IntelEz was introduced. In a way, they were already posthumans before they were subjected to the drug."

"Yeah, but that leads back to some kind of environmental factor causing the primary mutation in the first place."

"Yes, you're right, but perhaps we can isolate the initial mutation and recreate it. That would allow us to create our own posthumans."

"Is that what we're doing now?"

"Lotti always saw that as one of our prime directives," Dr Menker said, and turned back to the computer monitors, effectively signalling the discussion was over.

TikTak continued on to Lotti's quarters. Dr Menker hadn't said anything he hadn't known before, at least not about Elize. He wondered if Dr Menker's last comment had been a roundabout way to state his loyalty to Lotti.

Lotti lived at the base. She saw no reason to make a distinction between her life and that of the group. To her, they were the same thing. At least that was what she used to say. Tom's offhand revelations put her in a very different light. He knocked on her door and when there was no response, he tried it. It was open.

He found Lotti in the bedroom, reading a report, whilst blasting an electronica rendition of some famous classical masterpiece. TikTak couldn't stand it.

She looked up from the report, ready to lash out at whoever was disturbing her, her stern expression softening as she realised who it was.

"Tann," she said. She insisted on using his birth name in private. Another thing he didn't like. He had long since stopped being Tann Tak.

"Are you still running the show?"

"Yes, why do you ask?"

"Marksman told me you were on your way out."

"I'm still here, as you can see. Was that what you wanted to talk about?" She sounded almost disappointed.

"I want out," TikTak said.

He had Lotti's attention now. Her expression hardened.

"And why is that?"

"This isn't about the future of mankind any longer, just personal agendas."

"You always were naive," Lotti said dismissively. "Everyone has their personal reasons to be here. You too."

"Call it what you want. That doesn't change anything."

"You can't leave," she said with such finality. "You are needed."

"To do what?"

"You are key to everything that is happening. Your father is holding Elize. You brought in Tom and gained his trust. Without you we'd have nothing. We need you to get Tom to talk. We need you to find Elize. We need you." She tilted her head to one side. "I need you."

"I will help you," TikTak said, ignoring her last remark, "but once we've found my father, I'm done."

"You are done when I say you are," she said, her tone leaving no doubt she meant what she said.

TikTak nodded. He had expected to hear something like this, but had hoped for something different. His only way out was to run, and he wasn't willing to do that just yet.

"I better get on with it then," he said.

"You could stay here," she said, the invitation obvious.

"I've got plenty to do," TikTak said, and shook his head, knowing she'd extract some kind of revenge later for denying her. He turned to leave. "Tom needs his Omni Device back, by the way. He says it'll help him locate some information."

Lotti threw it over to him. "We've already made a copy of it. It's all encrypted. I don't want to get heavy-handed with him, but if I don't see results soon, I might have to."

TikTak left without answering. It had been a pointless threat, but telling nonetheless. She suspected some kind of link between him and Tom and wanted to find out just how far it stretched. The question now wasn't so much if he was going to run, but when.

He turned on Tom's Omni and saw it had a message waiting. Without unlocking it there was no way of telling more than that. It could even be one from his father. He hurried back to the upper floor to the room where Tom was sleeping.

"I need you to unlock this for me," he said. "You've got a message."

Tom sat up and stared at him bleary-eyed.

"Really? You wake me up for that?"

"Unlock the bloody thing!"

Tom took his Omni and held his finger against the touchscreen. Tik-Tak shook his head – he was still using a thumbprint as passkey. It was notoriously easy to break that. Tom then tapped a few times on the screen seemingly at random before checking the screen. *At least he had a secondary security measure,* TikTak thought, but it wouldn't take Dr Menker and his people long to break through it.

"I do have a message," he said, and frowned, "but it came the way you send me messages. It's just from a nearby device."

"Who is it from?"

"It doesn't say. I think it's just someone playing around."

Tom held up the screen for TikTak to see.

I need your help. Elize's body is in danger. Meet me at the attached location tomorrow at 4pm.

The attached location was a longitude and latitude. TikTak memorised them. "Yes, I think you're right," he said. "Someone just having fun."

TikTak had a look at the device id the message had come from. It was his own Omni. Someone was using it to relay messages to Tom. TikTak had no idea how that was possible. He was beyond diligent with securing his device. He had customised his Omni presence in the network from the firmware up, running obscure modified open-source agents to ensure it was virtually impossible to hack, yet someone had done it. It was almost as if whoever did it was making a point. The only person TikTak could think of that could have sent the message was his father, but he lacked the skill and wouldn't have written the message that way.

"So I can keep it?" Tom asked.

"Yes, we need to find out where Elize's body is. We have to find her before anyone else. Anything you can do ..."

"I'll see what I can do," Tom said.

"We've got a timeline."

"I'll see what I can do," Tom repeated with a grin, and put the earphones into his ears and lay back down on the couch. TikTak wondered if Tom had taken any other precautions to secure the information his Omni could access, not that he could do much about it. He just had to trust that Tom was paranoid enough to be prepared.

TikTak left the room, guessed that Tom was continuing to listen to Adrian's recordings. He hurried back to his own small room and started putting together a list of his father's friends and acquaintances. He had an ulterior motive this time. He wanted to run each of them against the location he'd been given before handing over the list to Lotti. He no longer wanted to help the group.

He made two lists. One with all possible connections: friends, anyone he had communicated with via private or company accounts, anyone from his private address book, anyone with even a hint of a connection to his father. He soon had a list of over a thousand names. It would take days for a Pattern Analyser to dig through that, which was exactly what he wanted. He then made a much smaller list of people he could remember his father having dealings with. He figured the person

his father had contacted had to be from his days in the hospital, someone he trusted, but might not have been in touch with for a long time.

He accessed a Pattern Analyser and loaded his father's name, the
list of 20 names and the location, and sat back. It estimated a completion time of 94 minutes. He sent the larger list off to Emerus Lorre, Dr
Menker and Lotti, apologising for the size.

Ninety-four minutes and counting. What could possibly go wrong
in such a short time?

10

Purpose – now that is something hardwired into humankind in the most ridiculous way. Once you get past survival of the individual and the society he or she is part of, what possible need do you have for a purpose? But if we don't have a purpose, we create one either consciously or unconsciously and then charge full steam ahead or hide from it.

I knew all this, yet I still could not completely ignore the urges it created in me. I began a self-study to keep my mind occupied with other things. I cast my mind back and let the tapestry of connections enlighten my past. Apart from the past few years, it was not even worth the bother. The singular thread hardly made any twists or turns on its inevitable way back to my birth. We have no concept of our real potential and my life made this painfully obvious. However, if the path to the starting point of my life had been a disappointment, the possibilities from birth were the absolute opposite – a singular bright light with almost infinite possibilities, reduced to a single path and finally fizzling out into nothing. In front of me lay all the possible paths my life could have taken. I stepped through my life, minute by minute, examining every inane thought and uninformed decision one by one. At every turn there was a vast sea of alternate options, almost all with a better outcomes. I had led such an average existence; it pained me to view it with any degree of clarity.

I watched my younger years with its carefree existence. Two simple concepts summed them up: egocentricity and the path of least resistance.

I had no issues with the former. This is who we are. In many instances it can be translated into a centricity around the closest group, such as friends and family. In some rare instances, it can even become a caring for a society or the common person, but I believe this to be an abnormal development, probably caused by childhood trauma. It is natural to care for yourself and for the ones close to you. Any extended care beyond that comes from other sources, but if is to be regarded as natural it has to be based on the ability to trace back a seemingly random act to your own wellbeing. Altruism, however commendable, is abnormal.

The latter – the path of least resistance – was something altogether different. It was natural for sure, but together with egocentricity it fostered a mediocrity that ran like a common theme through my life.

It was even worse as I progressed further in life. I managed to find a wife who wanted to share her life with me and it took me less than three years to squander it. In my estimation, the path of least resistance is the most common reason why most marriages come to nothing. And why shouldn't they?

The idea that someone can find fulfilment in only one other human for the rest of his or her life is a fallacy forced upon humankind by religion. We get stale, bored into a comfortable lull that can only be broken by introducing more people into the mix. I introduced affairs and one-night stands. She introduced girlfriends, each more annoying than the next. Without knowing it, we were both expanding our worlds, worlds we could live in because we weren't happy with our current shared one.

Don't get me wrong. I loved her. I still do. However, love only gets you so far and it wasn't far enough for me. Our love didn't give either of us stimulation. It just gave us someone to share the dullness.

She discovered my transgressions. We tried to patch things up, but our two separate worlds collided, making any reconciliation impossible. Her girlfriends – well versed in the unfaithfulness of men – soon became a bigger problem than the women I had had on the side. According to them, I had proven myself unworthy. If I had done it once, I would do it again. Whilst true, I hated their interference. I knew that two of them had had affairs, but somehow this did not disqualify them from having opinions. My wife and I parted ways not long after.

It still hurt. With all my knowledge and the ability to make sense of the world now, it still hurt. But in that emotion I also found my purpose. Whilst I had let emotion sweep me away, my mind had been busy creating connections. I existed in a vacuum. With all outcomes known, what possible interest could life hold for me? Sure, there were less probable paths to attempt, but they were all known states with known outcomes.

This wasn't strictly true, of course. There was an element of randomness I couldn't foresee and potential shifts in parameters that could have unexpected consequences. However, in the same way that ants in enough numbers can be irritating and make you move from one spot to another, it wasn't affecting me much more than that. The randomness was a nuisance, nothing more. So how could I break out of this vacuum? What could there possibly be that gave me a reason to get out of bed in the morning?

I was a race of one. The ants around me provided little more than momentary distraction. If I was to go on, I needed someone else like me, an equal to share experiences far beyond what Homo sapiens could begin to imagine. This was to be my quest: to create an equal. The religious implications weren't lost on me. Even with my godlike status, I couldn't determine whether an actual God existed or not. If there was such an entity, perhaps the universe was just a cry for help – a lone creature's desperate attempt to create an equal?

So now that I had my purpose, it raised two immediate questions: "Who would join me in godhood?" and "How do you change someone to be like me?"

I knew who I wanted as my companion. I had failed her once, and here was my chance to make things right. Elize was the obvious candidate.

How to do it proved a much more difficult question. It took me over two months to determine how to change her. I turned my intellect to determining what I was now and was surprised to find I had already started changing. My subconscious had begun a reconfiguration of what I was – a body to match the intellect it housed. It hadn't even occurred to me until now that I could examine my body and its automatic processes in much the same way as I could examine anything else.

What a marvellous machine it is, and yet so flawed.

It took only a cursory examination to question the possible involvement of a creator in its design. The mystery – if there was one – was how we had progressed this far at all. The spine was a prime example. It was an amazing construction for movement, but was obviously not for walking upright. Mine was reinforced, limiting movement somewhat. This was an understandable trade-off. Most of my physical enhancements, I discovered, were to better protect the brain and basic movement, which limited agility somewhat.

As I studied the different layers of the body, I found adjustments everywhere.

My metabolism had changed. I was now a hybrid with an organ specifically designed to store energy to feed my ever-increasing mind. Instead of allowing high-energy food such as sugars to flood my system, it stored them like a battery and released them as needed.

I had already seen the difference in analytics and critical thinking. The brain is an amazing organ, but to deal with the constant barrage of data and make sense of it, it filters, fills in the blanks and makes assumptions. My brain no longer did this. Instead, it processed all information, made all the necessary connections and fed the result into the probability matrix.

The most surprising changes I found were in the building blocks of who I was. A completely new process was reprogramming my genome using designed viruses as the tool. A new organ created viruses and released them into the body. It changed the cell by infecting it, reprogramming all the cells in my body continuously. It was correcting deficiencies in my DNA.

To my disappointment the endocrine system remained intact. Hormones were still coursing through me, manipulating my every move. At least the analytical mind was now better equipped to keep this somewhat in check, cancelling out some of the unnecessary base responses.

Amazing as it all was, this was not what I was looking for. All of these changes had occurred once my mind had already changed. I was after the genesis stage – what had caused the change in the first place.

It took some time, but in the end it wasn't very complicated. The change was caused by a number of completely unrelated small mutations working in unison with the introduction of IntelEz. It wouldn't be hard to create a drug that would create these different mutations. Anyone could become me, it seemed, but that was the last thing I wanted. Wasn't that the downfall of humankind anyway? Out-of-control reproduction using up all the available resources, spawning wars and conflict over the few resources that were left. No, a new race would be based on restraint, else we would be no better than the humans preceding us had been.

I created the drug and one night whilst she slept I administered it to her.

Elize, the mother of a new race.

11

Insurgence

Marksman had grown increasingly tired of the posturing. He thought the time for political positioning was long gone. They had control over more than three-quarters of the group's leadership, yet he had to wait. Emerus Lorre, leader of the opposition group, didn't want an all-out war, preferring a bloodless shift of power over a full-blown revolution. Marksman struggled to see the sense in that. Surely a clean cut was better than keeping the cancerous growth.

He looked at the list TikTak had sent and that Emerus had passed on to him. It was a joke. It confirmed what he already suspected: TikTak's loyalties lay elsewhere. Marksman didn't know what TikTak hoped to achieve with this little stunt and he didn't care. However the takeover happened, there were a select few he'd remove from the picture whatever Emerus said – TikTak was one of them.

Emerus was heading in the right direction, but not far enough. The new world would grow from the ashes of the old one. Their job was to fan the flames. It was in the ensuing chaos that a new world order would emerge. This wasn't a change that could be managed by committees or controlled with project plans.

"Are you listening?" Emerus said impatiently. He was standing up, staring at Marksman. Emerus was imposing. Almost two meters tall and solid. He had been quite the athlete, playing rugby at the national level, but had let himself go. Still a formidable foe though.

Marksman sat up. He had heard it all before. Political this and political that.

"And stop playing with that," Emerus continued, pointing at the tactical baton in Marksman's hands. "It makes me nervous."

Marksman smiled, but made no movement to put it away. "What are we doing here?" he asked the others gathered, before Emerus could continue. "What are we waiting for? We could take over this place tonight if we wanted to. We know who'd go with Lotti and could easily remove them."

"We all know what you think," Emerus said with a sigh. "The takeover requires planning. There is a subtle balance of power within the group. Once it changes, we need to make sure we can restore it – otherwise, we won't have a group left."

"Subtle balance?" Marksman said, trying hard to suppress a sneer. "The balance of power at the moment is that Lotti has it and we don't. You all heard the private investigator. She's whored herself out to any cause that'd take her. Is that really what we want? Even her own supporters will be asking themselves if she's the right person to lead the group. We need to move now."

This wasn't the first time Marksman had challenged Emerus on the takeover strategy, but so far he'd been unsuccessful. He had a feeling this time would be different.

"He's right," Jim Arkham said. "We've prepared for this long enough. Everyone is questioning Lotti's claim to leadership. We'll never get a better chance."

Marksman was surprised Jim had spoken up. He'd never before challenged Emerus and he knew Jim spoke for sections of their group that usually remained silent.

"We should wait," Emerus persisted. "If Lotti's leadership is under question, so much the better. She will be convinced to leave without us having to do anything. We have the majority and it will be a smooth transition, just the way we planned."

Marksman looked at the others. Usually everyone would nod as Emerus laid out the plans. This time no one did.

"No more waiting," Marksman said. "We've been handed a golden opportunity and we'll take it. There are a few people that will have to go, but that was always the case. We've been planning this for ages. We all know what to do. We should move now."

Marksman knew he had won and in doing so had taken a giant leap up the food chain. Now there was the question of how to capitalize on it.

"With your permission, I will deal with Lotti and her closest supporters."

"What exactly do you mean with 'deal with'?" Emerus asked.

"I will make them disappear," Marksman said. "Does it matter how?"

"They should be allowed to leave if they want to," Emerus said.

Marksman raised his eyebrows and looked at the others. They didn't say anything. Marksman loathed their weakness, but knew he had to work within the limits, or he too would be out. He'd put in a lot of work to rise within the ranks of EvoII, and he wasn't going to abandon the cause now. He needed to change the playing field, and the takeover of power was the perfect time to do it.

"In ten minutes I will move to have Lotti and her closest associates locked up," Marksman said. "I need you to control any information flowing to your respective groups. We move now."

They stood up and hurried out of the room. There was a sense of purpose in the group he had never felt before. Once they had all left, he turned to Emerus. "Could I talk with you in private? I just want to make sure it is all going in accordance with your plans."

"Your plans you mean?" Emerus said with a sneer, but still motioned for him to come along as he headed for the door.

"We are all after the same thing," Marksman began.

"No," Emerus said, and shook his head. "I doubt we share the same goal. Before the posthumans, I always thought machine intelligence would outstrip us in a few decades, and in all likelihood would have spelled the end for humankind. That all changed with Adrian and Elize.

They are the glorious continuation of our species. I suspect that to you they are no more than a meal ticket."

"You're wrong," Marksman said, equally annoyed by the accusation and the time he was wasting. "Give me a chance to change your mind."

Emerus studied him for a few seconds then shook his head. "No, it's too late for that. Once this is over, I want you out."

Marksman glanced up and down the corridor. Behind Emerus was a door into a small meeting room. It was closed so he didn't know whether it was occupied or not. He decided to chance it. He grabbed hold of his lapels and pushed him backwards through the door, making sure he was off balance so he couldn't use his superior weight to stop the movement.

He was in luck – it was empty.

"Let go of me!" Emerus yelled. He pushed Marksman away and crouched into a boxing stance. Marksman struck him in the throat with a knife hand, hoping to incapacitate him, or at least shut him up. He'd wanted to do this so many times. He wanted to savour his fear and pain, but he didn't have the time. He needed to get this out of the way quickly and focus on Lotti. If everything worked out as he planned, Jim would take over as number one. That would give him enough control over the operative part of the organisation to set his own plans in motion.

He'd planned this a long time. He knew Emerus had a partial heart replacement. It could be accessed wirelessly to change settings and Marksman had long ago acquired a hack to change its function. The manufacturers had thought of this of course and supplied its customer with jamming devices they hung around their necks that stopped any wireless signal. Marksman pulled open Emerus' shirt, located the jammer and pulled it off. He didn't like killing like this – it should be up close and personal. Sending a hack code to stop someone's heart didn't give any kind of satisfaction. He felt embarrassed as he instructed his Omni to activate the hack. Just as triggered it, the door opened, revealing one of Emerus's aides. Marksman didn't know his name. He had him mentally tagged as Fat Bastard because he was overweight. He had no respect for people who ate themselves into an early grave. "Have you seen …" Fat Bastard started, and then saw Emerus on the floor, still gagging from the strike on the throat. "What happened?"

Marksman looked down on Emerus. The hack was supposed to be quick. It overrode the security protocols and forced the pacemaker to race until the heart stopped.

"He just fell over. I've been trying to get help," Marksman said, pointing at his Omni processing wristband.

Fat Bastard sat down on his knees next to Emerus, an elaborate task requiring a number of adjustments and grabbing hold of chairs. Midways through this procedure Emerus half sat up and grabbed his chest.

"There's something wrong with his heart!" Fat Bastard said, and immediately started checking Emerus's pockets. "If I can find his Omni, I can run the diagnostics on it. He showed me how."

Marksman watched as Fat Bastard located the Omni. He realised then that he wouldn't get away with it – he was still holding the jammer in his hand. Fat Bastard spent a few seconds looking for it and then glanced up at Marksman. He knew. Still he kept going, running some kind of diagnostic function. This wasn't going to be the clean kill Marksman needed, but he didn't have a choice. What was worse, if Fat Bastard had an integrated Omni, he could have already sent a request for help.

Marksman pulled out his tactical baton and flicked it to full extension. He struck Fat Bastard across the back of his neck. The force of the blow threw his head backwards. Marksman swung the baton in an arc over his head and struck across the obese man's exposed throat. Fat Bastard sat there a few seconds gagging and then fell over onto Emerus. Marksman knew he would only live as long as the air in his lungs would allow. He checked Emerus, who by now was all but dead.

It would have been so much better if it had looked like an accident. Now it was a murder and someone had to be accountable. He knew he'd be at the top of that list, along with Lotti, from the group's perspective.

He could run, but it wasn't his style, nor did the situation require it. He had worked too hard to give up now. This was still salvageable.

First things first. He left them as they were, one lying on top of the other. On his way out he jammed the door.

He found Lotti in one of the group rooms. Dr Menker was briefing her about the discoveries so far. He called in backup and whilst waiting for them to arrive listened to the conversation.

"We've not gotten anything from the copy we took of Tom's Omni. There are encrypted parts in the solid-state memory, restructured to look like a regular files. If we hadn't started opening those files, we wouldn't even have known they were there. We've begun analysing them, but we suspect they are only partial files and that small bits of them will be stored in different infoDeposits. We don't even know if we're going to be able to get anything out of it at all. I wasn't expecting such security measures. Are we sure this guy is just a private detective?"

"Are you saying he's a government agent?" Lotti asked, glancing at Marksman, but not acknowledging him.

"I don't know what it means. He has stuff that looks like agent tech. He knew background information about you hardly anyone knows. Could he be some kind of undercover operative?"

"We should ask him,' Marksman said.

"He won't tell you anything," Dr Menker said.

"I can make him talk."

Dr Menker grimaced. He was weak just like the others. Not prepared to take their beliefs to their natural conclusion. EvoII would be better off without them.

"I don't think it will be that easy," Lotti said. "He doesn't have long before he's a deadhead. This is a cause for him and he's got nothing to lose."

"So what then?"

"TikTak is working on him."

"You can't trust him," Marksman said.

"I know," she said, just as Marksman's backup arrived. "And it seems I can't trust you either." She eyed the people behind Marksman. "Can't do your own dirty work?"

Marksman would have preferred to remove her from the picture altogether. As long as she was alive, she'd cause trouble. He didn't have that option now.

"Lotti. We no longer believe you are suitable to lead our group. Come with me."

"No," Lotti said, and stood up defiantly.

Marksman shook his head. She still thought she was speaking from a position of strength. She was going to make her case here and how. Marksman didn't think she'd succeed, but he wasn't taking any chances. He struck her hard in the face, open-handed.

"Take her and put her with the private investigator. They have lots to talk about. Anyone else?"

No one moved. Marksman wasn't surprised. They were weak. They followed anyone showing strength, whether they agreed or not. He loathed them.

12

Under Siege

Tom pulled the earpieces of his Omni out as the door opened. Lotti was pushed into the room. Tom almost laughed. But once she had regained her composure, she acted as if she were a queen under house arrest. She was attractive, with long blonde hair, blue eyes and high cheekbones – a model of northern European beauty. But her face never relaxed. She was like a coiled viper, always ready for the attack.

Lotti gave him a stare and sat down on the floor across from the couch. She nursed a bad bruise on her cheek.

"How did you know about me?" she asked.

"Trouble in paradise?"

"Trouble you've caused."

"You've been digging that hole for yourself perfectly fine without my help."

"How did you know about me?" she asked again.

"You haven't hidden your information that well. Anyone with a bit of time on their hands can find it."

"Why?"

"You know my background. You should be able to work it out."

She shrugged her shoulders. "It doesn't matter."

Tom returned her shrug. They sat in silence for over a minute.

"It was the IQ killings, wasn't it?" She held up her finger to keep him quiet. "You must have been assigned to the case as a detective when you were on the police force. I knew I was a suspect. I didn't realize how thorough you'd be."

Tom smiled. He had investigated her as part of those killings. It had been after Adrian had disappeared from the public spotlight, but before the full truth was known about the Drug. Six well-known public figures were competing for the spot Adrian had left. They were killed over a period of a few months. Lotti had been the spokesperson for a group of black-hat hackers that claimed they knew who the killer was.

"And now here you are. A bit too much of a coincidence, don't you think?"

Tom just smiled in response.

"So who are you working for?" she continued. "It can't be the police, but maybe you were recruited by another government agency afterwards?"

Tom shrugged. He saw no reason to let her know it was indeed a coincidence, and not a big one by any stretch. He had a number of cases focusing on homicides related to group activity. Her name – or one of her aliases – had come up more than once.

"We never found the IQ killer, so technically you are still a suspect."

"Whatever."

They sat in silence for a few minutes. Tom had no interest in her. Her own group had ousted her and from what he had seen of her so far, he didn't like her very much.

"Is it true?" she asked.

"Is what true?"

"Your killed your daughter once she became a deadhead?"

At first he didn't answer. He didn't necessarily want to discuss this with Lotti, but he knew her type. She would keep going until he told her – just to shut her up. Most of it was a matter of public record anyway. His case had become the precedent for mercy suicides for deadheads.

"Why?" she prompted.

"Because she asked me to."

"So why the thefts? I ran a social summary on you before you came. You were some kind of big deal as detective."

"She was in and out of clinics for over a year. Expensive clinics. It seemed a good idea at the time. No one would miss some of the money from evidence seizures."

"But they did."

Tom nodded.

"So your wife left you?"

"That happened as soon as my daughter was diagnosed. My daughter and I were very close. I was the one who had put her on a high dose of IntelEz. I was using it myself and figured it couldn't do any harm."

"God, it sucks to be you."

"You happy you know everything now?"

"I knew it already. I just wanted you to relive it by telling me. Revenge for outing me, if you like."

Tom laughed. The revenge was so disproportionate to his supposed crime that his mind couldn't come up with an appropriate response to her statement.

"So now we are stuck in here, the two of us," he said finally. "I think they put us together as punishment."

"I will be out soon. I still have enough supporters."

"The fact you're in here with me shows you don't."

"They're hoping I'll get something out of you. I won't, I know. You don't know anything more."

Tom smiled. "Since I'm still alive, someone thinks I do."

***

There was still 15 minutes left of the 94-minute running time of the Social Analyser when the door opened. Marksman entered with Erin and EpicL behind him. They all eyed him warily. TikTak knew what this meant. He had run out of time. He was surprised to see EpicL there. Someone had to replace Zemer, but EpicL was muscle and not much more. TikTak scanned them. According to his integrated Omni, EpicL's weapon augmentations were at full power. He was obviously expecting trouble.

"I want to know everything you know. Now!"

"I've told Lotti everything. Ask her."

"I will. But now I'm asking you." He glanced over his shoulder. "Hold him."

TikTak knew that each of them was his equal or better in a fair fight. He wouldn't stand a chance against all three of them. Better to save his strength and wait for an opening. It wasn't much of a tactic but it was all he had for now.

EpicL grabbed his hands, held them behind TikTak's back and twisted viciously. TikTak had nothing to match the power of EpicL's augmented muscles.

"I know how tough you are," Marksman said, "and I don't have time to break you down. I've been told this will do it for me."

He held up what looked like a high-tech helmet. TikTak had never seen one before, but he knew what it was. Full Virtual Reality had never hit the mainstream, but the military industry had found other uses for immersive technologies. The helmet was a sensory deprivation device. It controlled sight, sound, smell, taste and airflow.

"I hate crap like this, but I don't have time to get information from you the old-fashioned way."

Marksman pushed the helmet over TikTak's head. It was completely dark. Soft pads formed themselves around his ears and two plastic pipes went up his nose. A spout pushed against his lips. TikTak held his mouth shut, refusing to surrender to the helmet. The helmet made a few more attempts to push the spout into his mouth before delivering an electric shock that made it open involuntarily. It was all the time it needed to push the spout deep into his mouth. A soft, sponge-like material sealed off his nose and mouth. He held his eyes shut, but it didn't help. The helmet was hooking straight into his integrated Omni implants, playing a test pattern directly on his lens. He was completely shut off from the world outside.

Strange flavours, smells and sounds filled his world. It wasn't directly unpleasant, but he knew the device was just calibrating based on his reactions. It ended after a few moments, leaving all his senses in the dark – no smell, taste, sound or visual stimulation at all.

A sudden sting on the neck took him by surprise. He didn't know if he was being injected with a drug or not. Maybe the sting was just another attempt at calibrating the device.

The sudden sensory onslaught that came after was impossible to prepare for. Strobe lights pierced his retina, a high-pitched metal against metal screech looped back and forth, favouring his more sensitive left ear. The smell and taste of vomit overwhelmed him. He body convulsed. His mind was no longer able to tell the difference between the outside stimuli and its own state. However much it tried to purge its system from anything unwanted, nothing came. He kept convulsing repeatedly.

His world went black again and he welcomed it with all of his being. His body slumped in the chair, drained both mentally and physically. Why was he here? What was this place?

"This was just a taste of what is to come. Tell us what you know and it all ends."

Memory came flooding back. Marksman was torturing him for some reason. He didn't have any information worth knowing. How could he make this all stop if he didn't have anything to tell?

"A shame. I'll see you at the other end."

From then on, the world TikTak knew was no longer. His mind was in freefall, the sensory overload so disorienting he couldn't even imagine a world without it.

***

Mr Astin flicked between the video feeds. All positions were ready to go. For a brief moment he considered informing his superior, but de cided not to. Astin had delivered precious few results and couldn't afford anyone else taking credit for the operation.

It had seemed such a simple task. Locate and secure at least one of the posthumans. As soon as he was given the task he had operatives scour the online world for traces of them and very quickly realised this wouldn't yield results. The posthumans didn't try to hide their online activity, because they knew the quantity of communication they generated was beyond the capability of any normal Pattern Analyser. He suspected they generated a lot of this activity to hide their true intentions, but whatever the reason, it had made standard techniques useless.

He had hired private investigators, people who still held on to the old notion of investigation work, to counter this. It was mainly older cops and agents trying to make a living outside the force and agency. Tom was one of them, and his methods – whatever they were – paid off very quickly. He had soon located the female, Elize.

Mr Astin had decided to have her followed so they could take both of the posthumans at the same time. Adrian and Elize had begun their war and he'd reasoned he'd be able to take them both during one of their battles. In retrospect, this had been the wrong call. He should have brought Elize in immediately. Tom had proven much less loyal and much more resourceful than he had expected.

Now he had nothing and Tom was the only one who seemed to know anything about the posthumans' whereabouts. The only way to recover this operation was to bring him in and find out what he knew. He had tried at Dr Tak's office, but hadn't expected EvoII's involvement. Now it was likely to get messy. He had faith in the teams doing the extraction, but it didn't matter. Even with all his planners amped up on IntelEz, complications were bound to happen. EvoII wasn't much of a threat. They did have some ex-military members, but it was unlikely they'd put up much resistance. You never knew what fringe groups such as EvoII would do. He didn't expect them to go suicidal and blow the place up, but he couldn't completely discount that scenario.

He watched the video feeds as the teams began. They entered the building from the front, the roof and the parking garage. It didn't take them long to secure the front entrance and the entry into the garage. The team entering from the roof weren't as lucky. A makeshift barricade stopped them and they had to disassemble it before proceeding. The original plan was to have the team entering from the roof do the extraction, whilst the others would hold their positions. If more obstacles slowed them down, they'd have to take an alternate approach. He hoped not, as that would likely turn messy.

The team secured the area as they progressed down one level in the building.

Mr Astin watched the progress and listened to the secured audio frequency the troops used. He smiled. Finally something was going his way.

"We have five civilians outside the building." The report came from the team in the lobby.

His smile immediately disappeared. If they were EvoII members this would very quickly turn into a gunfight. He checked the video feed from the team in the lobby. They didn't look like EvoII members. One of them was even wearing a hospital gown. They just stood outside and watched until the sliding doors opened of their own accord.

"How did they do that? We locked those doors!"

"Just get rid of them."

There was something strange in how they moved. Mr Astin didn't know what triggered his unease, but their blank faces and almost robot-like movements made him nervous. If they weren't EvoII members, then who were they?

The woman in a hospital gown smiled and walked up to the reception desk where two of his men were posted. The others had taken positions, ready to step in if need be.

"How can I help you?"

The woman kept smiling, pulled a gun from under her hospital gown and shot him in the face.

The other attackers reacted immediately, running towards the positions where the other operatives hid.

"We have a hostile approaching here too. Only one that we can see." This time the report came from the parking garage.

Mr Astin ignored it, watching as the attackers were disposed of. They didn't have much in the way of weapons – another handgun and an assortment of knives – but they wielded them with such complete disregard for their own safety that they were dangerous nevertheless. He suspected they were on some kind of drug.

"Secure the door!"

One of the operatives ran towards the door and jammed it.

"There are more of them out there."

The audio link from the garage suddenly went dead. Mr Astin swapped to the video feed to see what was going on. At first he couldn't make out any details. He rewound half a minute in the video feed and watched as an obese man walked up to the position held by his men. He smiled and waved at them as he approached. They told him to stop, but he didn't listen. Someone fired. A flower of red appeared on the man's chest, but he kept going until he was close. He looked at the camera and winked. A second later he exploded, taking the team out with him.

Mr. Astin couldn't believe what he was seeing. The attackers behaved like terrorists, happily sacrificing their lives. As he watched the video feed from the garage he could see movement. Through the dust there were the outlines of more people entering the building.

He swore as his Omni alerted of an incoming anonymous private feed.

"Who is this?" he snapped.

"Are you currently attacking EvoII's headquarters?"

"It is an extraction of a key resource. Tom Devine knows where Elize is. I need him to locate her."

"We have already secured Elize, and from what I can see it is a slaughterhouse. Get them out of there."

"That order can only come from my direct superior."

"Consider him outranked. This is Leonid March."

Mr Astin sat back down. Leonid didn't just own the company, he owned the corporation of which this company was only a small part.

"I'm taking over this operation. I want the extraction team out of there now. Let Tom Devine go."

Mr Astin studied the video feeds again with growing dismay. What had started as a nuisance was now an all-out attack. He had been keeping an eye on the nutcases in EvoII for months now, but he had never expected this. An all-out attack by what looked like a rival group.

"I don't think that is possible any longer," he said, and hung up, knowing he no longer had a job.

13

Wipe out

TikTak reconnected with reality like a careering car meeting a brick wall. He realised this was the real torture. The sensory deprivation was so severe that the mind went into a fugue state to deal with it. Once it was gone there was no longer anywhere to hide. His head pulsated, as if the electric pulses in his brain had been multiplied a hundredfold. He had lost count of the times it had stopped and then started again. He just knew there was no escape.

Suddenly the spout in his mouth retracted and the helmet loosened its fit somewhat. He blinked but it was still completely dark. White text blinked in the right upper corner of his vision: *Sensory overload program B.9 complete.*

He realised he could hear distant voices, so he focused on that as his body screamed its pain. He could only hear snippets of conversation.

"Someone cut the power ..."

"We're under attack ..."

"... find out what's going on ..."

"... keep an eye on ..."

TikTak just sat there. Time no longer meant anything as his mind struggled to make sense of a muted world.

Suddenly the helmet was yanked off his head, almost ripping off one of his ears with it in the process.

TikTak slumped in the chair. He knew he needed time to regain his grip on reality.

"Wow. It really did a number on him, didn't it? How long was he in there?" It was a male voice, harsh and cocky.

"Fifteen minutes. Maybe less." A female voice. It sounded distracted, maybe even nervous.

Fifteen minutes. The time meant something. He focused on it as a lifeline and it delivered. The Social Analyser had fifteen minutes left when he was captured. It would have a result that might lead him to his father. With this rediscovered purpose, TikTak pushed the pain away and tried to compartmentalise it enough to think clearly. Someone was attacking the EvoII headquarters, but who? Probably the same crowd they had met at his father's clinic, but why attack? They knew Elize's body was somewhere else, so there had to be a different reason. Tom! They were after Tom. He swore to himself for not working it out quicker. He had to get out of here.

Marksman had left them already, leaving the two voices he had heard – Erin and EpicL. He knew he couldn't beat EpicL in a fair fight if it didn't involve weapons. It didn't matter though. EpicL had augmentations to increase strength that were hardwired into his integrated Omni. TikTak had hacked that many months ago for just this eventuality.

Erin was a different question altogether. Her, he could take on unarmed, but she already had her gun out and she was a good shot.

They were both standing in front of him. EpicL hadn't bothered tying him to the chair, preferring to flaunt his superior strength by holding him in place. Now that Marksman was no longer there, he had let go, positioning himself between TikTak and the door.

"Who's attacking us, you think?" EpicL asked Erin.

"Government agents. Fascists!"

TikTak prepared a message for Erin, tagged it with Marksman's signature and sent it. He hoped she'd just act and not analyse it.

Erin froze.

"I need to go,' Erin said and headed for the door "You OK here?"

"This little guy? Not a problem."

As soon as she left, TikTak stood up. "Let's see how tough you are."

EpicL raised his arms and frowned. "What have you done?"

"Let's see how tough you are without enhancements."

EpicL sniffed. "I don't need them to deal with you."

TikTak knew he was right. Even without enhancements he was still a much better unarmed fighter, but TikTak had no intentions of fighting on his terms. He had thrown his baton on the bed when entering the room and it was still there. He had to go through his adversary to get to it. EpicL was in a boxing stance. He usually favoured striking.

TikTak feinted a side knee kick, easily blocked EpicL's clumsy counter strike and moved to the side. He had become used to his augmentations. Without them he was slow and uncomfortable. EpicL followed up with a jab feint and then immediately followed up with a front kick to the abdomen. TikTak let it hit him but turned even more, letting the force push him in the direction of the bed.

"I'm going to kill you," EpicL grinned.

He still had the grin when the end of the baton struck him in the temple.

TikTak sat down. He'd been lucky. The pain from Marksman's treatment was still clouding his thoughts. He knew he didn't have long and now he had to deal with Marksman's people and whoever was attacking EvoII. He accessed the motion surveillance system he had set up over the past few weeks. A map of the building appeared in front of his eyes and he could see any moving bodies as glowing dots. Most of the EvoII members were already tagged, but he could see another fifteen or so spread out, some on the lower level and some coming from the top level. They had secured the exits and were moving in, securing the building room by room.

He could still get to Tom before them, but getting back out was another question entirely. He started running. He needed to get to the stairs before they were secured. As he ran, he started questioning why he was trying to rescue Tom at all. He had the coordinates, which was the best lead to find his father. Tom was going to be a complication, since everyone was trying to capture him.

One of Marksman's goons was half running towards him. In the dimly lit corridor, he didn't even register who TikTak was until they were side by side.

"You ..." the goon started, as TikTak hit him with a side sweep to the back of the head. TikTak grabbed his gun and ran up the stairs.

From the perspective of saving his father, there was no point in saving Tom. But there was a bigger picture here. However much he despised what EvoII had become, he still believed in their cause. The posthumans were humanity's only hope. Tom, for reasons he still struggled to understand, was the most likely link to either of the posthumans.

From his internal map he knew there were no hostiles on this floor yet, but they were coming. He ran to the room where Tom was held and unlocked the door. To his surprise both Tom and Lotti were there, glaring at each other. Lotti looked ready to punch Tom.

"We need to go," TikTak said.

"What's happening?" Lotti snapped at TikTak.

"We're under attack. They've already secured the top level and the entrance. We need to find another way out."

"Who's attacking us?"

"I don't know. We have to go now!"

He mapped out potential exit points whilst the invaders, appearing as unidentified dots on his retina, crept closer. The front entrance and the roof were blocked off. There were numerous windows on this level. He could probably climb down from there, but he wasn't sure whether Lotti or Tom would be able to do it. More than likely, snipers would pick them off anyway. There was an entrance to the car park at ground level, but it was also secured. There were a few other options, but they were in areas already occupied by hostile forces. He could see no option but to fight their way out.

They heard shots fired from the lower floor. It seemed the bulk of the hostiles were entering from street level. He decided they had a better chance to escape from the roof.

"We'll go up. There are two other buildings we can reach from there, but we need weapons." He handed the gun to Tom and watched as he checked it. He kept forgetting Tom had a past in the force. "We'll have to pick some up on the way."

They hurried towards the stairs. To TikTak's dismay, he could see the hostiles were getting reinforcements. More and more dots appeared at ground level. It wouldn't be long before the building was in their hands.

They ran up two flights of stairs and as they entered the upper floor, he swore. He hadn't had enough time to analyse the movements. The reason the hostiles weren't moving was that some of the EvoII members had managed to block the key corridor that went like a spine through the building. They had built a pile of office chairs and tables and anything else they could find almost all the way to the ceiling. They stood on one side, hiding in door openings, while the hostiles were on the other side. It was effectively trench warfare.

He didn't think it would take long for the hostiles to break through, but until they did the three of them were trapped.

He sat down and analysed their options again. They had to get out of the building somehow. He checked the lower floors and was surprised to see there had been no movement into the building. There was activity for sure, but it seemed the hostile force had been stopped in their tracks. Even more attackers were entering the building as he watched.

The building shook. Something had exploded further down in the building. It must have been on the garage level, as there was no immediate change in movement patterns at ground level.

Chaos reigned on the ground floor and he instantly knew why. A third party had entered the fray and was sending more and more people in. He quickly explained the situation to Tom and Lotti.

"Our best bet is to get out in the confusion. It's dangerous as hell, but I don't think we have a choice."

"Why are they attacking?"

"They're after you!" TikTak couldn't believe how dense Tom was.

"I don't think so. What are you guys doing here? EvoII, I mean? Anything anyone would want?"

"We don't have time for this. We need to go now."

"So we are going to walk to freedom through a three-way gunfight?" Lotti shook her head. "In that case I'll need a gun."

"There'll be plenty where we're going."

TikTak again took the lead. He had no idea what to expect on the ground floor so he tried to make sense of the little information he had as they descended the stairs. The motion surveillance system could no longer decipher the movement, and just reported a mass of moving bodies. To his surprise, there were still more people coming. The first attack had been clean. A small number had gone in and secured all the exits and then methodically went through the building. The second attack was very different. There was no skill or method to it. It was an attack by someone with superior numbers and no regard for the lives of their rookie troops.

The fighting was no longer restricted to the lowest floor. Three people in civilian clothing chased an injured man in full combat gear up the stairs. They pulled him down and slit his throat with what looked like a kitchen knife. One of them looked straight at TikTak and he realised she was a member of EvoII. She smiled. It was the last thing she ever did. One of the other attackers plunged the kitchen knife through the back of her neck. She fell forward.

TikTak shook his head. They were not agents. The one closest to them was an overweight man in his mid-thirties, with food stains on his sweaty clothing; the other, a petite woman in a hospital gown, her head shaved. TikTak figured she was fifty years old. They were not on the agents' side nor were they with EvoII.

He struck the overweight man over the head repeatedly. TikTak was surprised how much damage he could take before he fell to the ground. The petite woman was lying at the bottom of the stairs, hit by a stray bullet.

They made their way past the bodies in the staircase. The petite woman grabbed hold of Tom's leg as he stepped over her.

"You have to get out," she said, blood spurting from her mouth as she spoke. "I will help you."

She held on for a few more seconds before slumping into a heap. Tik-Tak checked the overweight man and found an old Omni in his back pocket. He took it, hoping it could provide some explanation as to what was going on.

He scanned the chaos in the wide hallway. Injured and dead, both agents and civilians, lay on the ground. What at first had seemed an impossibility now looked doable. If they moved quickly they had a chance of getting through.

"Stay close behind me," he said and ran.

Perhaps it was just luck, but they were almost halfway down the corridor before he had to get involved. Two EvoII members came towards him, one armed with a bowie knife. TikTak struck the knife hand, shattering the wrist. He pushed the attacker into another fight and turned to the remaining man, who now backed away.

He continued down the corridor, again surprised at how easy it was. He struck a few people out of the way, but no one challenged them until they turned the corner and could finally see the foyer of the building. This was a larger area where civilian bodies lay in piles. Agents still held it, firing at anything entering the building. The sliding doors were jammed open by bodies on either side. A glass wall and the open door were all that stood between them and the attackers.

As they approached, they could see movement from outside. Ten or more people were charging the glass wall with bricks and pieces of metal. They began battering the wall and circular patterns bloomed like flowers where they struck.

Someone suddenly grabbed his arm and started pulling. He had no idea how anyone had managed to get so close to him, but realised it was Tom who was falling to the ground. He checked him for wounds, but found none.

"What happened?" TikTak asked.

Lotti shrugged.

"Help him. He's having an episode." TikTak couldn't think of any other reason.

"He's a dead man walking?"

He nodded. "He should be able to stand and walk. You'll have to lead him."

"Just leave him."

"Don't you get it? They're here for *him*!"

She stared at him defiantly for a second, then crouched down and struck Tom twice in the face.

"There you go. He should be with you in no time."

TikTak shook his head, but could see that her action had the desired effect. He hailed a car, in the unlikely event they made it out alive.

The glass in the vestibule was designed not to shatter, but to remain in sheets even when broken, but it didn't matter – the sheets of glass were coming away from the frames from the sheer force of the blows. As soon as a gap opened, the attackers started welling through.

It was clear the agents hadn't equipped themselves for a fight like this. They had expected a covert extraction and ended up in trench warfare. They managed to stop the first wave of attackers, but another came soon afterwards and stormed their positions.

"Are you ok to make a run for it?" TikTak asked Tom, who was trying to stem the flow of blood from his nose.

"Yeah, I think so. What happened?"

"You had an episode."

He nodded. "Let's go."

They ran past the few remaining agents and attackers. To TikTak's surprise, there were hardly any attackers left on the street. He could see onlookers further away, but no one else ready to fight. The last surge of attackers must have been the final wave. It all seemed just a bit too coincidental.

The three escapees entered the car that was waiting for them.

14

Adrian's Audio Clip #4

Emotion. Well, there is another useless concept. Humankind is already beyond the stage where emotions and their results serve any real purpose. This was a twofold discovery as I watched Elize unfold into my equal.

I had a painless birth. She wasn't so lucky. Through a fortunate roll of the dice, I had been born with the required mutations; Elize had not. I administered the drug over five nights, recreating the mutations one by one. It shouldn't have affected her in any negative way, but she still came down with an infection and ended up sick for weeks. This wasn't completely unexpected, but frustrating, regardless. Most likely it was an infection that had been in her system before I even started the process.

Two weeks later, I ensured she took IntelEz. She was an intermittent user anyway, using it to cope with her personal life. This, I understood, was a common use of the Drug for women. Instead of antidepressants, IntelEz was used to gain clarity in the emotional turmoil that was everyday life.

My world suddenly opened. Her reactions and behaviours were unknowns. Remember, my first reaction to the Drug was to climb down the face of the building. I tried to determine the logical progression of events from this point, but the uncertainty at each point had suddenly doubled or tripled. What I really needed to do was analyse the reasons for this and adjust my approach, but I was too excited, my vast analytical ability nullified by the emotional reaction to finally having begun my plan. I wanted her to know the wonders the new world had to offer. This was my first mistake. One of many.

Perhaps some more context is in order before I continue. Elize left me six years ago, and within months had found someone else. A year later they were married. She was now a stay-at-home mum with two young children.

I waited for her husband to leave in the morning and then knocked on the front door. Her reaction as she opened it baffles me to this day.

"Adrian, what have you done?" – the first words she'd said to me since our divorce was finalised. She knew there was something different about her, and seeing me she immediately concluded I was the reason.

She invited me in, but only after I asked. She was holding her one-year-old son, who was obviously in the middle of his breakfast, as he was wearing most of it. I recalled the ideas I had about eliminating the child stage from the development of our new race. They were such an ineffective, messy way of furthering a race.

I told her I had made her like me, and again I could hear the religious analogy echo in my ears: "I have made you in my image." Was this how God felt when finishing the Creation? I'd like to think so.

Elize wasn't impressed, and I had suspected she'd react like that. I had considered asking her first, but the likelihood of her acceptance was less than ten percent. This way the success rate was just shy of fifty percent. It was a strange conversation, where she provided both sides of the argument. She kept asking questions and then immediately answering them herself, as her mind kept supplying the most likely scenario. She negotiated the questions until she stopped for a moment to consider the why, but that too soon occurred to her.

"Adrian, how could you? I don't want to be like you."

I remained silent. This was the make or break and there was nothing I could say that would increase the chances for her to join me. It had to be her conclusion, her decision.

"And I don't want to be with you."

My heart stopped. All my planning had led up to this moment and I had failed. The only answers I had, I had calculated to have less than a ten-percent chance of changing her mind, so I stayed quiet.

She asked me to leave and I agreed, telling her she would see things differently once she had had time to explore the gift I had given her. This I knew to be true. Once she understood the full impact of what she had become, a completely new baseline scenario would begin.

I was right, but only partially. A week later, I visited her again. According to my calculations, this was the optimal duration needed to develop an understanding of her position beyond the immediate future.

She let me in this time and studied me dispassionately.

"I guess I should thank you," she began, carefully choosing her words. "You have changed my world for the better. I never thought I'd say those words to you, so thank you."

I nodded, impatient for her to continue, impatient for the new world to begin.

"I also know why you did it. And my answer is no."

Her answer sent a shockwave through my probability matrix yet again. I had no idea how to respond to her rejection whilst it adjusted.

"Please leave," she said, and saw me to the door and closed it after me.

How could I have been so wrong? The probability of rejection had been less than one percent, yet here I was. It didn't take me long to realize that I hadn't been wrong at all. After all, I wanted purpose, a challenge beyond what humanity could muster. She promised to give me both. I was certain that given time she would make the right decision.

I watched her over the next few weeks as she carried on with her small, pointless life. Diapers, baby food, trying to get the baby to sleep, pushing a stroller to the park to meet other equally pointless mothers. Husband comes home from his pointless job and they spend the evening fussing over their pointless children before putting them to bed and then falling asleep in front of the TV. And repeat. And repeat.

How she could find any satisfaction in such an existence was beyond me, yet she persisted. I had given it a week until she gave up on her pathetic existence, but two weeks later nothing had changed. I grew weary of this game. She would join me. It was only a matter of time. All paths on my probability matrix led to that point, but some of those paths lasted years. She needed a push in the right direction to speed things up, and I knew exactly how to do it.

Her husband took the two children to toddler play at the local swimming pool. On their way back, I arranged a driverless car to malfunction and ram their car into the opposite lane. None of them survived.

15

Revenge

Tom pulled the earpieces out. He felt sick.

Tom had seen old interviews and Adrian had always been charming and smooth. On these recordings he was anything but. What was the point? Why had Adrian left these files for him to find? Apart from getting to know the real Adrian, which was a mixed blessing, there had been one important revelation. Posthumans could be created. This was the secret everyone was after, the reason he had been hired to follow Elize in the first place. If that information was in there, the search for the posthumans no longer mattered. However, it all came back to the reason for these recordings. Adrian had planned all this.

Tom laughed to himself. He was like an ant trying to understand the magnifying glass that was slowly roasting it to death.

"Finally off your relaxation tapes?" Lotti said.

"I find I don't have to listen to you if I pretend to listen to something else," said Tom. He watched the sunrise through the car window. "Where are we going?"

"I ran a Social Analyser on my father," said TikTak, "and ran the resulting profiles against the location you were sent. There was a match on a Leonid Marsh. He's a doctor, worked with my father in the army.'

Lotti frowned. "You got one name from that list of yours? There were thousands of names on it!"

"I used a different list."

"Traitor."

"To whom? I didn't like where EvoII were heading."

"The military?" Tom sat up. He didn't like that at all. When the downwards spiral began, many of the military organisations rejected the lead of their governments and became semi-autonomous. "We don't want to mess with the military."

"Don't worry. That was long ago. He's disgustingly wealthy. Built a company around biotech and now spends most of his time saving the world."

"You think he's an ally."

"Could be."

Lotti snorted. "He's no ally. We've come up against his people more than once. He's the competition."

"Who is he?" Tom asked.

"How can you not know who he is?" Lotti asked.

"Generally, because I don't care."

Lotti shook her head. "PharmaCom introduced IntelEz in the first place. They were small back then, but quickly became a world player. Leonid was behind releasing the patent so other companies could make copies. He wanted the whole world to benefit from it."

Tom did know this, but had never thought too much about who owned what. In his mind, large companies were entities in their own right, great beasts with their own agendas. Who owned it never entered the equation.

"You should look up the speech he made when the patent was released. I watched it live and remember thinking he was an idiot. Guess he proved us all wrong."

"How so?"

"Check out the speech. It will be on the feed."

Tom located a public feed that had the speech on his Omni. It was a ten-year-old news report, snippets of a longer speech glued together with an over-excited reporter attempting to provide commentary.

"Leonid March, owner of PharmaCom and the man who gave us IntelEz, hit the business world with a bombshell this morning. In a press conference, he announced that anyone could now produce the Drug."

Leonid appeared on-screen, a grandfatherly figure with well-groomed greying hair.

"I have decided that IntelEz is too big a discovery to be held up by patents and red tape. It will herald a giant leap in the development of humankind and it is not right that a private company should own it. I've just signed the paperwork to release all our information about the drug to the world. I give the right to anyone to produce the drug."

The journalist again appeared on-screen. "The move was commended for its generosity, but Mr March ended the press conference with a warning ..."

"IntelEz is one of the greatest advances of our time, but it is also our greatest threat. Even though it has passed all the tests, I'm concerned about the biological and societal implications of this drug. Now that everyone has access to our information, I'm hoping that research is conducted far beyond what our company can do. Will it be our death or our salvation? It is in all our hands now."

"Reactions from the business world vary," the journalist said, "with many suspecting it's an elaborate ruse."

A business commentator sitting next to the journalist added, "Mr March is portraying himself as a modern-day Jesus, but I'm not buying it. There is a bigger play here that we're not seeing yet. You don't just give away a discovery that could generate billions. There is ..."

Tom closed the feed and sat back. If this was the man they were up against, it didn't matter if he was a friend or foe. He had unlimited resources, and once he had what he wanted, his plan would be all that mattered. Tom couldn't do much about that now, so instead he tried to understand the attack on EvoII's headquarters.

"What happened back there?" Tom asked. "I think I know where the agents came from, but the others? They looked like civilians."

"Hang on ..." TikTak dug an old Omni from his pocket and tossed it to Tom. "I took it from one of them."

Tom opened it and the home screen immediately appeared. No security measures at all. It was an old model and the operating system hadn't been patched in over a year. Tom scanned the usage profile and found nothing out of the ordinary. The owner had used it sparingly. He went back to the membership profile.

"He was a deadhead," Tom said.

"No, he wasn't. I saw him fight. "

"He's got a food administration id."

"Show me." TikTak took the Omni and flicked through the profiles. "He was a deadhead," TikTak finally agreed. "How is that possible?"

"Mankind is evolving," Lotti said.

"How do you mean?"

"Perhaps what we call deadhead is a pupation stage, a preparation for a new development. Perhaps we will all become like Adrian and Elize. I don't know." Lotti shook her head. "I'm tired of all this. It looks like what we were fighting for will happen anyway."

"And that's a bad thing?"

"Everyone becoming posthumans?" Lotti sat back and grimaced. "If everyone is special, then no one is. How is that a good thing?"

"So it's all about being special?"

"Isn't everything?"

"Even if you're right, why attack EvoII?" Tom asked.

Lotti shrugged.

"It wasn't an attack," TikTak said. "Or at least it wasn't an attack until the other party arrived."

"What does that mean? I saw them killing EvoII members too."

"If they're becoming posthumans, who knows why they do anything," Lotti said. "We are no more than bugs to them."

"So you still think this was an extraction attempt? They were after me?"

TikTak nodded.

"Why?"

"I'm still working on that. Help me out here."

"I think the soldiers may have been sent to get me, yes. I was tailing Adrian and Elize for PharmaCom."

"And you tell us that now?"

"I didn't really trust you until now."

TikTak paused for a second as if to digest his comment and then shrugged. "If Leonid was trying to get you, aren't you basically delivering yourself to him now?" said TikTak.

"I don't think that message came from Leonid. I think it came from your father or someone working with him. And nothing I can think of explains the other group. One of them said something to me. Something about getting out and that she'd help me. She died, so not sure what that was about."

"It doesn't make any sense."

"Bugs." Lotti stared out of the window. "We are all bugs to them."

Tom gave up. He was too tired to care. It would still be hours until they reached their destination. A car directly behind them drew his attention. The network ensured the traffic flow with mathematical precision. This car was too far away from them and not exactly in the centre of the lane.

"Get off the main road and then back on it again," Tom said.

"Why?"

"We're being followed."

"How do you know? This car isn't even on the network."

"Just trust me. There are many ways to follow a car."

"What do you mean? Satellite? A tracker? Hacking our drive computer?"

Tom smiled. "Or they could just manually follow the car."

"You mean drive it?"

"Yes."

"Why would anyone ..."

"Just do it."

The car they sat in suddenly veered right into a side street, and then two more right turns to take them back to their original route. The car behind them followed them around.

"You're right," said TikTak, "we're being followed."

"Do you think there are many or just this one?" said TikTak.

"He's on his own. If he's driving by himself, it's because he doesn't want to tell the network to follow our car. The ADN is easy enough to hack, if you know how. Someone with resources wouldn't follow our car like that. They'd just hack the ADN. We need to get rid of him."

"Hang on."

TikTak sat back for a few seconds. The car behind them suddenly stopped.

"What did you do?"

"I reported him for drink driving. He has to agree to let the ADN take over."

"But won't he just instruct it to follow us?"

"I'm hoping he will. Now leave me alone to do this."

Tom watched TikTak as he stared glazy-eyed into nothing. Tom hated what the world had become. Never before had people been more connected and never had they been more alone. He knew this was the old world watching the new world with disdain, but he couldn't help himself. For all our advances, we were still just cavemen. TikTak was the perfect example. He was obviously some kind of hacker, but at the same time he wielded a baton to defend himself.

"Lotti, what's the story with TikTak?"

"Ask him."

"He's busy doing whatever it is he's doing."

Lotti shrugged. "He was one of Marksman's hacker contacts. Marksman must have seen some promise in him beyond his computer skills, because he brought him into the group and trained him. That's why they both fight with T-bats."

"T-bat? Those sticks they both use to fight?"

She nodded.

"So what did you do?" Tom asked.

"Is it that obvious? Marksman and I never saw eye to eye. I took Tik-Tak from him. He's never forgiven me for it."

Suddenly the car stopped.

***

"The ADN will now take over control of the vehicle," a soothing female voice said. "What is your end destination?"

Marksman let go of the wheel and sat back.

"Don't lose them," he said to KimEra on over a private feed.

"I've got three bots tracking them," she replied, with a bored autonomous tone. "They're going nowhere."

This was the first time he'd used her as part of an operation and he wasn't impressed. Sure, she followed orders, but never anything else. TikTak had been the only hacker he'd actually enjoyed working with. It didn't matter what he asked, TikTak had already thought about it and explored alternate options. It didn't matter any longer – he was on the opposing team now.

"Where are they going?" This was the third time he'd asked and he had little hope of actually finding out.

"He's given it a circular route with multiple stops and five handovers to other vehicles. It's impossible to determine ... shit!"

Their car slowed down.

"Whatever happens, don't lose them."

"He's reprogrammed our vehicle. He's convinced the ADN that our car has a dangerous fault. It will return to base. I've got a replacement vehicle coming, but it will take a couple of minutes."

"We don't have that. Sort it out!"

"And he's disabling my bots one by one. He's good!"

For the first time Marksman could hear actual emotion in her voice. She sounded like she was having fun. He'd never met her, but from the research he'd done before hiring her, he knew she was one of the best, and would only take on jobs she regarded as a challenge – in this case, the opportunity to go up against TikTak.

"I know he's good! You're supposed to be good too."

"He'll get away if I don't ..."

"Don't what?"

***

The car in front of them stopped and the lights turned off.

Marksman watched as Lotti, TikTak and Tom left the car and headed for a nearby industrial complex.

"What did you do? Why did you stop their car?"

"He killed my bots and was about to re-route this car. I had to do something."

"So you failed," Marksman said.

"How did I fail? They're right there! I'll send you the route he programmed."

Marksman could hear the excitement in her voice. From her perspective, she had stopped TikTak so she had succeeded.

"Do you seriously think that would include the end destination?"

"No," she said, after a while.

He shook his head. "Find them for me. Now."

"Give me a minute."

"You've got 30 seconds."

Marksman had a look in their car. Apart from some fresh blood-stains, the car was clean. One of them might be injured, but not seriously. He had seen them exit the car and there had been no sign of injury then. He didn't want them injured. He wanted them dead. He had to keep reminding himself that they were a means to an end. If he was going to locate any of the posthumans, they were his only lead.

An incoming feed from KimEra. She had better have something.

"The industrial area they headed for is abandoned. It has surveillance systems and many of the machines in the factory have sensors. I can activate their accounts and start it all up. It should give you enough time to locate them."

"Do it."

A few seconds later, the factory came to life as if workers were lined up outside its gates. Abandoned sites – even complete areas in cities – were more and more common. Production output from the world at large had fallen to about half that of the golden age. They remained wired up, ready in the unlikely event they would be needed again.

"Give me a trace of their route."

Markers appeared in his view. They had entered the main gates and headed for the office connected with one of many larger factory buildings.

"It will take me a minute or so to trace them from there," KimEra said. "Some of the machinery is still dormant."

"What kind of factory is it?"

"House printing, I think."

Marksman laughed. No wonder it was abandoned. The population was decreasing and deadheads were collected in institutions. If anything, they needed fewer houses, not more.

He waited patiently while KimEra surveyed the sensors to determine where they were. He wasn't interested in hunting them down inside the building. It would be both dangerous and counterproductive. He wanted to track them to wherever they were going.

"They entered the building and then went into the main factory area. From there I can't see them. Either they're still there or they've disabled all the sensors."

"So you're saying they're hiding in there?"

"Most likely, yes."

"Or you aren't as good as you think."

He didn't get a reply and hadn't expected one. She couldn't care less what he said. Every time he asked her to do something, she received a payment in advance.

"But they're not in the office building?"

"No, they definitely left. I can trace a basic id tag hack and three people leaving shortly after."

"Can you start the machinery inside?"

"Sure. I'll load some designs and kick it off."

He entered the office building, following the markers in his view. He didn't trust KimEra, but he didn't have a choice. If he was going to play a role in this, he couldn't lose more time. The big boys had entered the fray and he couldn't compete with their resources, at least not for long.

"Can you hook me into the feed from the surveillance system?"

"Sure. Won't do you any good though. He's disabled it."

"TikTak?"

"I'd say so. The security sensors on the machinery are still operational, so if they trigger any of those I'll know. I've also started the warehouse robots in case they try to escape that way."

"Ok. I'll find them."

"They're still somewhere in the factory or warehouse. All doors leading out of the building have operational sensors."

It was all a matter of time. If TikTak had enough time, he'd be able to hack a door or other exit without triggering any alarms. Marksman couldn't let that happen. He had to keep the pressure on, force them to make mistakes he could exploit.

He opened the door that led from the office building to the factory. The two buildings were connected by a small corridor that opened onto a large factory floor divided into eight sections, each holding a printer large enough to print a bedroom in one go. This was a print-on-demand factory able to produce a house in less than a day. He had seen a printed building go up in two days once the foundation was laid.

Six of the eight stations were printing something, but from what he could see through the protective screens it wasn't a room.

The furthest two were sounding alarms. Marksman expected them to be decoys, meant to delay him. He didn't have choice though; he had to make sure they weren't hiding there. He pulled aside the protective screen of the first one. There was no place to hide within the printing station. In the middle was the beginning of a sculpture of some kind. A three-by-one-meter base and four large feline paws, ending abruptly.

Marksman approached the second printing station.

"I've picked up movement in the warehouse," KimEra said. "The pick robots have motion sensors to prevent accidents. I'll send you the coordinates."

Marksman quickly pulled the protective screen aside. The same statue base had been printed here, but apart from that, nothing. He knew TikTak was just stalling. With enough time, he'd come up with a way to fool KimEra.

He ran through the enormous doors that connected the factory floor with the warehouse. He was surprised at the size of the building. Usually, any kind of printing industry was purely on-demand, and required very little warehouse space, but it was of no consequence – he would push them hard enough that they wouldn't have time to cover their tracks.

He ran towards the coordinates KimEra had sent earlier, entering a section of the warehouse with narrow, maze-like corridors. He turned a corner and stopped. A small pick robot was trapped under a crate, attempting to free itself. Marksman knew it was a trap. Someone would be waiting for him along the corridor of crates.

He moved slowly, trying to assess where the attack would come from, when a shot rang out and a bullet ricocheted on the concrete floor next to his foot. He threw himself back against the crates on the same side he thought the shot had come from.

It made no sense. Why attack here? He knew they were following a trail leading to the posthumans. They couldn't afford any delays, which meant this was some kind of diversion.

He looked around and saw a bigger pick robot come down the corridor, metal arms aimed at his chest. The bulk of the robot took up most of the corridor width, leaving him with few options. He jumped up and climbed the wall of crates, barely escaping the robot arms. It turned and extended its legs to follow him as he spidered up the crates.

"KimEra," he said over an active voice feed. "What are you doing? I'm being attacked by a robot! Shut it down!"

The pick robot had almost caught up with him when it stopped, arms reaching towards him, metal claws extended.

Marksman took a deep breath, then another shot rang out. This time Marksman could see where it had come from.

"Send the pick robot five meters down, the same side I am on, and have it start pulling crates out," he said over the voice feed.

The robot came to life again. The electric engine hummed quietly as it started down the corridor. He started climbing along the wall, using the robot as cover. It started pulling out crates and dumping them on the ground.

He saw movement from the gap between a crate and the shelf just above where the robot was. He let the robot pass the spot and immediately grabbed hold of whoever was in there and pulled.

Lotti came tumbling out from her hiding spot, falling two meters and e landing on the concrete floor at an odd angle, twisting her right leg. Marksman jumped down next to her.

"All the doors triggered at the same time!" KimEra's voice came through his earpiece. "I have no idea how he did that."

"Check external surveillance."

"It's been disabled."

TIkTak had beaten them again.

Lotti smiled, an obvious effort through the pain. "Never expected to beat you."

"I can get it up and running again," said KimEra.

"We've already lost them. Track any car requests from this location." Marksman looked down at Lotti. "I have something I need to do here."

He grabbed hold of her hair, wrapping it once around his hand, and pulled her along the floor through the warehouse maze. She grabbed hold of her hair to lessen some of the pain.

"I've wanted to do this for a long time," he said and yanked her hair hard.

She grimaced. "I don't care what you do to me. You've lost."

"I'll show you what losing looks like."

He dragged her along and into the printing factory. The printers had half-finished the statues. The four legs were complete and a muscular feline body was half complete. He grabbed hold of Lotti and threw her up on the level area that was still being printed. She landed on her back, her head tilted back beyond the printed statue. The printing arm immediately stopped, red warning lights flashing.

"Override the safety switches on the printer," he told KimEra.

"Sure," KimEra said, and then went quiet. "What are you doing?"

"I'm paying you. Just do it!"

The printing arm started again, but stopped immediately when it reached Lotti's arm. The heat from the muzzle of the printer made Lotti try and pull away. Marksman struck her arms with his baton, aiming for her elbows. She screamed, no longer able to move.

"Make it print around any obstruction."

"Sure, but it will stuff up my design."

"You're printing a Chimera. Not that hard to work out. Get on with it."

The printer arm started again, but this time it kept ejecting the hot plastic that immediately turned solid, following the contours of Lotti's body. She screamed as the plastic fused with her skin.

Marksman watched her as she slowly became part of the statue. She was still alive, but hardly tried to move any longer. Tiny whimpers escaped now and then.

Parts of her body were still visible. Her head tilted back, her eyes stared into space. He watched as life escaped and her body went limp.

Lotti was dead. He felt ecstatic, but somehow he had hoped for more. He had taken his revenge, yet he didn't feel as much as he had expected. He knew why. There were still loose ends to tie up.

"Wow!" KimEra said through the voice feed. "Now that is a statue!"

"I take it you have the surveillance system up and running then?"

"I do. Too late to locate the rest of them, but I have tracked ten vehicle requests. Mapping their destinations now."

"Send them to me. It's time to end this."

16

Elize Renewed

Dr Tak was tired. He hadn't slept since first laying eyes on his subject and had long since lost track of time. He didn't even know if it was night or day. He was repeatedly offered help and refused it every time. Elize had been his patient since Tom had delivered her and would remain so. He didn't trust anyone else.

He suspected he didn't have long. He now knew he had been wrong to accept Leonid's help. The fact that Leonid had initiated contact should have been the first warning signal, but at the time he had seemed the perfect ally. He had the resources to hide them and help them, and had been part of discovering IntelEz. Leonid had been nothing but civil and had accepted all his requests, but Dr Tak couldn't shake the feeling he was being humoured. It was as if they were just waiting for something to happen and when it did he would be removed. Permanently.

Dr Tak was now of the opinion Leonid was the person he should have hid from in the first place.

Over the past – *Had it been two days and nights?* – Elize had made a remarkable recovery. Her skin had regenerated, shedding the old burnt one like sunburnt skin. The new skin was harder, more akin to a reptile's, which made even taking blood samples difficult. Not that he knew what to do with them any longer, anyway. Most of her bodily processes had changed. She was still human, but only in the same sense that a Formula One car was a car. He suspected this was not a direct result of IntelEz, but a follow-on effect. The Drug had opened the door, but Elize was the architect behind the modifications, whether consciously or unconsciously. She had been killed, but managed to keep her body in a suspended state until the base functions could repair themselves and harden her body against any future attacks.

He couldn't do anything for her apart from keeping watch and documenting any changes. He kept logs to keep his benefactor updated on Elize's progress, but he also had an ulterior motive. IntelEz had promised, but not delivered. Adrian and Elize were the only known cases where IntelEz had lived up to its promise and the question was why. Along with each test he made to keep Leonid and his cadre of scientists happy, he did additional ones to determine the underlying cause of Elize's abilities. He knew it was an almost impossible task, and he had not had much success so far. Her internal organs and external characteristics were changing so fast it was difficult to locate any specifics that might have been the trigger.

He reached down to take another skin sample. Elize's eyelids flicked open and she grabbed his wrist in a vice-like grip.

"We're under attack."

Dr Tak just stared at her. This was the first time he had seen her in a wake state, let alone hear her say anything, so it took him some time to adjust.

"How do you know?" he finally asked, but regretted it instantly. He knew, or at least suspected, that she had many new ways to communicate with the world. Earlier the same day, he was questioned about the amount of net traffic he was generating. He had excused it with running sample data against medical databases, which was true, but that wouldn't nearly account for the load. He suspected Elize was directly tapping into the local network, which would give her access to security cameras, motion sensors and anything else installed in the facility.

Elize looked at him and nodded. "Help me."

Dr Tak helped her up into a sitting position. He knew she was strong, but her energies were diverted to other unknown purposes, leaving her with only basic abilities. At least this was his current theory.

He could hear the pressurised doors further down from the lab open.

"We need to hide you."

Elize didn't answer, but let herself be led to a hiding spot behind a medical cupboard. He knew it wouldn't hide her for long if they searched the area, but he didn't know what else to do.

Heavy footsteps rang through the corridor. It was Leonid's personal army on its way. That couldn't be good. He had only seen the soldiers once before, when he first came to the facility. Leonid had brought them along for safety, not knowing the extent of Elize's capabilities. Once he had seen her state, he had come on his own the next time.

There were ten soldiers. Dr Tak had been introduced to their leader, but hadn't taken much notice at the time.

"We are here to take the body," he said. "Where is it?"

"What are you going to do with it?"

"The body is no longer your concern. Where is it?"

"She's no longer here."

The leader of the group stared at him for a few seconds, a shark deciding whether to eat or not.

"According to the security cameras she woke up and you led her ..." He walked over to the hiding spot. "Here."

He stared at the location. There was no one there.

He turned around and aimed his gun at Dr Tak.

"Where is she?"

"I don't know," Dr Tak answered truthfully. He had expected her to be there as much as the mercenary.

"You are of no use to us. If she doesn't show herself, I will shoot you."

Dr Tak had suspected as much. He knew he didn't have long, and thought he had come to terms with it, but faced with imminent death he found he was not as prepared as he had thought.

"She's hacked your cameras. She could be anywhere by now."

"Maybe, but you've been looking around the room as much as I have. You expected her to be there too. My bet is she is still in this room."

Dr Tak shrugged in response.

"And that means we don't need you."

Dr Tak stared at him defiantly.

Two things happened at once, neither of them the shot that Dr Tak had expected.

The lights went out and the fire alarm sounded. There were no windows in the room, so once the lights went out, the only light source was a few pieces of older medical equipment that still had touch screens. As his eyes adapted to the low light environment, the equipment powered down. It was pitch dark.

Dr Tak ducked down and crawled towards the door. The mercenaries were shuffling around close to him. He could hear the growing panic in their voices.

"Get the lights going again! Anyone with a flashlight?"

"Comms is down, sir. There is some kind of interference."

"Hang on, I've got one."

A flashlight came on and immediately went out again.

"What happened?"

"We need to get out of here!"

"Door is not responding!"

"Force it open, hack it, just get it open. She'll kill us off one by ..." Dr Tak recognised their leader's voice.

No one moved for a few seconds, as they waited for their leader to say something. Anything.

Dr Tak had lost his bearings completely. He knew there was no point moving towards the door. From what he could tell from the voices, the mercenaries had all gathered around the door, so he crawled as far away as he could. He ended up in the far corner and made himself as small as possible when all hell began.

"She's here. She's ..."

Someone started firing. One bullet struck the wall next to Dr Tak's head. One of the mercenaries started screaming. Dr Tak just lay there, eyes closed, holding his hands over his ears.

He remained in that position until silence prompted him to open his eyes. The light was on. The ten mercenaries were dead, most of them with their throats ripped out, a couple with gunshot wounds. Elize stood frozen in front of the door, an angel of death, blood-splattered from head to toe. Dr Tak watched her. This was the future of humankind. A new race steeped in the blood of the old.

He knew he couldn't do much for her, but he'd do what he could. He examined her body, washing off blood in the process. She had a knife wound in her belly, but it had already stopped bleeding. He crouched down to examine it.

"It is not needed."

Dr Tak looked up and saw Elize watching him.

"We should go from here." Dr Tak said. "It isn't safe."

"It is now."

Dr Tak looked around at the bodies and shook his head. He didn't know what Elize meant, but he believed her. If she said it was safe, who was he to disagree?

"My body needs rest to rebuild. Watch over me."

She lay back on the bed she had spent most of her time on since they had arrived.

17

Reunion

The hire car drove into a small lane in an up-market industry district. From the architecture, it was obvious that all of the buildings had been completed in the past few years. House printing had let a whole new breed of building designers come up with outrageous structures. If it could be modelled and was structurally sound, it could be printed.

"We should have stayed and helped her out," TikTak said. "She won't stand a chance against Marksman."

"Would you?" Tom asked.

"In a fair fight? No."

The car stopped. "You have arrived at your destination," the vehicle informed them. "Your account will be charged. Please step out of the vehicle."

"This is it," TikTak said.

"So how long do you think we have?"

"I sent ten hire cars off in different directions. That should buy us some time, but not much. Marksman has found himself a good helper."

"Where are we, by the way?"

"It's registered as a research laboratory owned by a small private company."

"Yeah, right."

Tom's Omni beeped.

"I thought you had turned that thing off."

"I disconnected it from the network."

Tom checked his messages. A new one read: "Use main entrance. I will open."

"It seems we are expected," Tom said, and showed TikTak the message.

They approached the main entrance. The heavy metal mesh protecting the front of the building rose slowly. The lights inside flickered to life.

Tom pulled the door open and entered the building. Sliding doors opened behind an unguarded security checkpoint. For every turn they made, another door opened or light flicked on guiding them further into the facility.

"Who is doing this?" Tom asked.

"Would be easy enough if you had access to the main control server."

"So could your dad do it?"

"I doubt it." TikTak stopped. "Do you think he's the one sending the messages?"

"Who else?"

"Yeah, good question."

Yet another door opened and they walked into a larger room splattered with blood. Ten soldiers lay on the ground, killed by what looked like an animal. Some of them still clutched weapons. Tom took a few careful steps, trying to find parts of the floor without pooled blood.

Dr Tak was cleaning a body lying on a hospital bed surrounded by medical equipment. The body was Elize.

"What are you doing here?" Dr Tak asked, not even bothering to look up.

"Who did this?" Tom asked.

Dr Tak nodded towards Elize. She looked so serene, more like a victim than a perpetrator.

"Is she injured?"

Dr Tak shook his head.

Tom couldn't believe it. She had killed ten armed mercenaries with her bare hands. It didn't seem possible. If she was capable of that, what else could she do? He remembered the section of the sound files where Adrian had spoken about how he had started reconfiguring his body. Maybe Elize had done the same. What else lay within her capabilities? She was probably the one who had sent him the messages. What could she possibly need from him?

"Tann, why are you here?" Dr Tak had finished cleaning Elize's body. A tower of bloodied towels was on the floor next to her.

"Someone led us here. We thought it was you."

Dr Tak shook his head. "You shouldn't be here. You and your friends. You shouldn't be here."

"I'm not with EvoII any longer. They were destroyed."

"Good."

Dr Tak stared at his son, challenging him to respond. TikTak just took a deep breath, looked down and nodded. Tom could see this was a sore point between them.

The door opened and another batch of mercenaries stormed into the room, weapons ready. Tom and TikTak soon found themselves on the floor on their bellies. They left Dr Tak alone, but three men were aiming weapons at Elize at all time. They also had night vision googles ready. Tom knew then how she had done it. The same way she could send messages to him. She was hooked into the control system of the building. She somehow was able to access the network directly without an Omni or any other technology interface.

She had turned the lights off and killed them one by one. The network provided her with enough information. Perhaps she could see in the dark. Tom didn't know what to think any longer. Her capabilities were a complete unknown.

The mercenaries carried the bodies out and made a cursory attempt to clean up the blood on the floor. Tom tried to speak to one of them, but got no response.

Ten minutes later, Leonid Marsh appeared. His head was shaven and, if anything, he looked younger than Tom remembered him from the old news report. Tom knew that recent research into ageing had made some breakthroughs, but to his knowledge none of those had filtered down to human trials.

Marsh looked around the room as if to assess the situation. Tom knew this was all for show. He would already have seen the state of the room through the cameras and probably also a light-adjusted copy of the actual attack.

"She is something else, isn't she?" he said, as much a personal musing as a statement to the people in the room. "I mean she really is something else. You can hardly call her human any longer."

"You were going to kill her." Dr Tak held her hand, like a father would hold a daughter.

"Oh, nothing so drastic. She was going to be moved to another facility where we can keep her in suspended animation indefinitely."

"What is all this about?" Tom asked.

"We've stared into space for intelligence beyond ours. We've built more and more complex machines hoping for intelligence beyond ours. We always thought the singularity would be external to us."

"The singularity?" Tom asked TikTak.

"There are people who believe machines will become smarter than we are. They call it the singularity," said TikTak.

"Seriously? Doesn't the whole IntelEz thing show that'll never happen?"

"That is indeed the case," Leonid continued. "We've become the singularity. Adrian and Elize have at least. And since you know what it is, tell me what the most logical scenario is when the singularity occurs."

"Intelligent beings will want to secure resources for their own species," said TikTak. "They will fight their competition for those resources – and we are the competition."

"And there you have it. Elize here – remarkable as she is – is the competition. She is the giant leap in evolution we never thought could happen. When I introduced IntelEz, I thought I had allowed us to leapfrog into the future. I knew there would be problems, but I also knew that we would be able to deal with them.

"Then came Adrian. He represented something different. He was a new species no longer bound by the same rules as everyone else. At first I thought he was an anomaly, a sign of where we might be in hundreds, maybe thousands, of years. I had this theory that evolution was a self-correcting mechanism not just for mutations that are not beneficial but also for mutations that go too far. Yes, a remarkable first in a species can occur, but the odds of another one occurring that could create offspring of the new species seemed a complete impossibility. But then came Elize, the perfect companion. It was almost as if it was planned, or maybe it's in our genome to trigger macro evolutionary leaps. There are many conflicting theories."

"You've really wanted to hold this lecture for a while, haven't you?" Tom said.

Leonid smiled. "I've held it hundreds of times at University, every time students start believing that posthumans are no real threat. But as you describe the scenario over the next few hundred years as a posthuman race is established, pretty much everyone changes their mind."

"So where does it all end up?"

"If we don't kill them now, they will kill us. Perhaps not directly, but over a few generations."

"So why isn't she dead?"

"I was going to. She convinced me otherwise."

"How?"

"She induced a coma in my granddaughter."

"When?"

"30 minutes ago."

"From in here?"

"She's taken over the local network. She accessed my granddaughter's Omni implants and overloaded them. I don't know exactly how."

"So shut down the network."

"She implemented a dead man's switch – if I mess with anything, many will die."

"Maybe she's bluffing?"

"I don't think she needs to. It took her a few seconds to compromise my granddaughter's implants and work out a way to induce coma. I'm sure she can design network agents that can do all sorts of damage. But it all proves my point."

"Which is …?"

"If we don't kill them, they will kill us."

The finality of that statement finally hit home. He was right. From everything Tom now knew about the posthumans, they would kill anyone standing in their way. Not of out spite or anything so mundane. They were true utilitarians. Whether a human lived or died made no difference to them when humans were so plentiful.

"So what's the plan now?" Tom asked. "Seems she is calling the shots, not you."

"She is. And she can hear everything I say. My plans will have to remain mine for now."

"She already knows."

"Yes, I guess you're right," Leonid said with a shrug. "I'm hoping she'll lead me to Adrian."

"What makes you think they are the only posthumans? Surely you've run statistics models showing otherwise?"

"We have. And yes, it is possible, even likely, there are more posthumans elsewhere, but we have to start cleaning up our own backyard first."

"Cleaning up?" Tom shook his head. "Killing our future, more like it."

"The world isn't ready for that future. Not yet."

"So you make that decision?"

"Someone has to look out for the human race." He turned to leave. "You are free to stay here if you want. There are a few rooms down the halls for sleep studies. I will make sure food is supplied."

"And if we don't?"

"That would be unfortunate, but it is your choice."

Tom knew what that meant. It would be unfortunate for them. They were prisoners, however politely it was stated.

Tom was beyond tired. He no longer had a concept of time or when he had slept last. He made his excuses and located one of the sleep research rooms.

The bed was inviting enough, but it didn't matter. His mind was in turmoil, the same kind of turmoil that had led him into using IntelEz more and more. He longed for the order and simplicity it created. Not amping up any longer had been one of the most difficult things had had done, and he couldn't stand the chaos. He knew everything fit together somehow, but without the Drug, his mind just couldn't cope with it. He also knew that if he wasn't careful his mind would find an arbitrary pattern and he would again suffer an episode.

He pulled out the last two of Adrian's sound files as a distraction. Maybe he finally would find out what this all was about, but he doubted it.

18

Adrian's Audio Clip #5

Primal urges. You are defined by them and the little window-dressing a cultured society and upbringing might have added. All your decisions can be traced to your need to fulfil those urges. So what happens when you redefine those urges? Being human is such a limiting condition.

I had developed far beyond my primal self, but in many ways I still had the same driving forces. I kept turning this over in my mind. I wasn't interested so much in what I was, but what I could become. I had been changed in some ways, but remained the same in so many others. What was the next step in what I could become? I found myself returning to this repeatedly.

My experiment with Elize had come to an abrupt end. At that point, I still had statistical reasons to assume she would join with me, but also that I would have to give her time. I had calculated the risk she'd turn on me at less than 10 percent, but that was exactly what she had done. I didn't blame her. She was acting in accordance with her nature. I blamed the model I had built. However, I was also refreshed by the idea I could be wrong. Of course, I had been wrong before, but this was different. On those occasions I had taken a stab at something based on the probabilities. The outcome didn't always go my way, but in close cases I always substantiated the probabilities and I was invariably right. Now I couldn't do that. Elize was an enigma to me. Her actions seemed almost completely random. She attacked me first. I hadn't even considered it within her capability.

I was in one of my many safe houses when an oil truck crashed into the building and blew up. She had reprogrammed it and removed all safety measures to ensure it would explode. I was lucky to get out alive. Do you know what my immediate response was?

Joy.

I hadn't been so happy since I had turned posthuman. Here was finally a challenge that evaded basic quantification. The news feeds have documented our ongoing battle, so I see no reason to go into detail about it, but it taught me a very important lesson. Nothing drove me to change faster than having to fight for my survival. Humankind has in some areas nullified evolution. When anything is acceptable, the weeding out process no longer works. Both negative and positive mutations spread, and believe me when I say the negatives far outweigh the positives. Evolution has stopped being a functional driving force on an individual level and has moved to a cultural and social playground. Here it is very much alive and this is where I found the answer. However, I'm getting ahead of myself.

Elize and I battled over many months, every action provoking a counteraction. I believe she enjoyed this game as much as I did. We both had the ability to kill each other many times over, but we always left an out, a way to survive if we were clever enough. We caused a lot of destruction and many deaths, but if myths teach you anything, it's that when the gods do battle, innocents will always be caught in the crossfire. The stakes were too high to worry about right or wrong, and I had long since stopped thinking in such terms. They are not the absolutes that religion would have you believe. They weren't even relevant concepts. If someone needs to die for me to survive, then so be it. If a thousand people need to die for me to live, then so be it. If you are not convinced of your own superiority, or at least your ability to achieve it, you do not deserve to live. There is nothing wrong with standing on the bodies of others to reach the highest goal. It is what we are and we should be proud of it.

But all good things must come to an end. I knew one of us would die if we kept going like that, and I could not afford it to be me, however much fun I was having. I also knew that the only way this could end was in an all-or-nothing scenario. The only acceptable bait for this trap had to be me.

And so I planned. The location had to be impossible to escape, so a bank vault seemed the best option. It would give her a false sense of security, thinking I had no way out. Of course she'd expect a trap, and of course there was one. I had rigged explosives to incinerate anything and anyone in the vault. Now there was just the question of how not to be in the vault when they went off.

I had a theory shared by quantum mechanics. I had designed a device that theoretically should move my mass through a fold in space to reappear in the same spot seconds later – basically teleporting on the spot. Being in one place and not, at the same time. This was an extension of the quantum teleportation that had so far only been done on sub-atomic particles in controlled conditions. I was convinced it was possible to achieve on a larger scale. I was willing to bet my life on it. In all honesty, I did have a backup plan. Whilst my body might be passing through quantum space, my mind would be elsewhere.

She came, but again you know this. You followed her there. My plan went as planned. I had noticed in our last few meetings that she preferred physical attacks. She had improved her physical characteristics to better deal with damage to a point where she was very dangerous, but it also spelled out her approach to attack. She'd want to get up close and personal. That was what I had counted on.

What I hadn't counted on was how fast she'd be. As soon as we made eye contact, she ran towards me. I triggered the device and the explosives, but too late. She had already reached me when it took effect and enveloped me into quantum space. She too became part of the entangled state.

My plan had been to incinerate her, but this worked out equally well. I had prepared my body for the quantum energies. She hadn't. Even with the protective layer, I knew it would be hell in there. The sheer force eroded my skin. Afterwards, my gut felt like it had been turned inside out, and in her case it would be a literal truth. Even if her body survived, her mind wouldn't. I had taken steps to protect mine. For the few seconds I was in there, my mind was safely hidden away.

When I returned from quantum space, both our bodies fell in a heap on the buckled, blackened floor. As my mind returned, I watched Elize's body for a few seconds. It had to be done, but I felt regret nonetheless. I had made her in my image for a reason, however ill-informed, and it saddened me to see her dead. She had been the only other one of my kind.

A second explosion rocked the building. This one much larger than the one I had set in motion. Not that it mattered. The building could collapse for all I cared. I had succeeded in what I had set out to do.

19

Discovered

Marksman stood outside the research facility and watched as an H-cell Mercedes departed. It was the fifth location he'd checked after KimEra had given him the destinations for all the vehicles TikTak had sent out. KimEra had spent over an hour determining the types of businesses near the location markers, so he had had to visit them one by one to decide for himself. Sure, he had asked her for classified facilities too, but it should still have been quicker than that. If he had known there was an unregistered research laboratory at this location, it would have been top of his list. Now he had lost hours tracking them down. Yet another reason not to use KimEra again.

It didn't matter. He was still on a high from killing Lotti. Now he wanted the rest of them dead.

He couldn't see anyone inside, but that wasn't surprising. It was Sunday, so he had no expectation of finding anyone there – at least none of the regular workers.

The light in the foyer was turned on, which was odd. The building's automation system should have shut it down; the energy preservation act demanded it. The departing car had come from the back of the building so someone must have entered the building recently.

He tried the door and found it unlocked. There was a reception area and two main doorways. He checked the reception desk hoping to find a switch for either of the doors. As he did, one of the screens came to life. It was the security camera for the front door. He guessed his presence had triggered the screen.

Controls on the screen allowed swapping to other cameras, including internal ones. Marksman flicked between the feeds at random and suddenly saw Dr Tak and TikTak talking to each other. Behind them lay Elize on a hospital bed. This was the closest he had ever been to one of the posthumans. Nothing else mattered. He would gladly give up the revenge he had planned for TikTak and the private investigator if he could secure her.

He kept flicking between feeds and saw a number of mercenaries posted throughout the research facility. The camera feeds gave locations, but they meant nothing to him without a layout of the building.

He swore to himself as he opened a feed to KimEra and asked her to locate a blueprint or plan of the building. At first, she just refused to do it. With the promise of double pay, she agreed, but only with payment in advance. Marksman wired the amount via virtual currency.

Ten minutes later, she had hacked the city planning servers and pulled out the blueprints. It didn't help much, as the cameras were named based on the names of rooms and corridors, which didn't appear on the blueprints.

He asked her to access the servers in the facility to see if she could find the building layout there. Another five minutes passed and an anonymous private feed came. He was surprised his Omni let it through; most anonymous feeds were immediately terminated by a screening agent he had loaded. It was KimEra.

"I don't know what these guys are doing," she said, "but you owe me a new setup."

"What happened?"

"The security system is crazy! Instead of denying access as most systems do, this one let me in and presented layer after layer of virtual processing units. There was no way to tell which was a real one and which was a dummy unit spun up by the security system, so I went through a few of them. When I exited to get some agents uploaded, I found my whole system wiped! I had to go and borrow an old Omni to get back to you now."

"Everything wiped?"

"Even my Omni processing unit! What are they doing there? I've never seen anything like it."

"Thanks. I'll take it from here."

"You owe me a ..."

He disconnected. He knew he'd have to repay her somehow; having a pissed-off hacker chasing him was the last thing he needed. The bigger question was who could wipe the systems of an expert hacker in a matter of seconds. There was only one answer to that question and that meant they already knew he was here, but the video feed suggested otherwise. Elize remained on the hospital bed and the two men still argued in front of her.

There were no real shortcuts to this. He reviewed the room Elize was in and tried to match it to a location on the blueprint. The most likely options were a number of large rooms, two floors below ground level. He couldn't see any obvious alternate path to get there apart from a back door, which led to the same stairwell as the front entrance would. There were two sets of lifts, but it was too risky to use them. He had no way of knowing what would be on the other side and had no way to retreat.

As he stood there assessing the situation, the sliding doors behind him opened. His pulse raced as he threw himself flush against the wall, baton ready.

No one came through and the door remained open. He had a quick look, but all he could see was an empty corridor. There was nothing wrong with the system, at least not that he could see. Either someone was helping him or it was a trap. He had begun to suspect that Adrian and Elize were still at their old war and that he had somehow ended up a pawn in it – one of them frying KimEra's equipment, with the other one helping him now.

Marksman entered the corridor and the doors closed behind him. Lights blinked to life like the solution to a maze. He followed them. Three turns later he almost walked straight into two mercenaries.

He scrambled back behind the corner he'd come from, sure he had been seen. He knew from the blueprints he was close to the lifts. The stairwell was in a corridor further ahead. There was no way around.

He pulled out a small camera and placed it so he could assess their position. It didn't take long to determine they were not waiting for anyone to break in. They were guarding the place to ensure no one got out.

He smiled. This would be easier than he had expected.

20

Adrian's Audio Clip #6

I have a grand plan to take humankind from this sad state of affairs and you are integral to it. I know you are deteriorating from the use of IntelEz. I know you have maybe six months left before you join the dead-heads. I have a simple question for you. Do you want to be like me?

I'm building a new race, but not everyone is capable of changing. You are. Deep in our genetic code are combinations capable of unlocking what I have become and maybe even more. Who knows what a thousand posthumans could do if they worked together?

The war with Elize taught me one thing. You cannot be a race of one or even two. I'm inviting you to be one of us.

Find me. You have my location in your hand.

21

A Riddle Solved

Another riddle. Tom hated riddles. He thought of them as a smug way of showing your superiority: solve this to prove you are worthy of joining our exclusive society!

Was this even a riddle he wanted to solve? He had set out to help Elize because it had seemed the right thing to do. Now, after listening to Adrian's ramblings and seeing the events of the last few days, he wasn't so sure he wanted to help them at all. At least not Adrian. He was dangerous. Elize was a different matter. He could still relate to her choices, even if they were extreme.

Then there was the question of becoming posthuman. He had been without IntelEz for the past month and he had struggled without it. If being posthuman meant keeping the clarity that came with the Drug then he would do it in a second, but could he trust Adrian? Tom knew he couldn't, but he had started down this road and wanted to see where it ended. He was, after all, dead soon anyway – might as well go out doing something that mattered.

So what did this riddle mean? To have something "in your hand" could refer to anything, but usually it meant something in the physical world. The more he thought about it, the more it seemed it wasn't a riddle at all. It was a safety precaution. The audio files could be copied and distributed to anyone, but the physical memTag itself could not.

He had left the files on the memTag to ensure that anyone taking his Omni wouldn't get the files. He dug around in his pocket and brought out the little device.

Initial study revealed little. It was about the size of his thumbnail but he couldn't see anything out of the ordinary. Such devices weren't very common any longer as most files were stored and shared through encrypted infoDeposits. If there was anything there, he couldn't see it.

Tom loaded the files into the secure scatter area in his Omni. This automatically split the files apart, encrypted and stored them across multiple infoDeposits. He broke the memTag open and looked inside. He didn't know much about what it should look like. There were small electrical components laid out like an aerial view of an oil refinery. He needed a location. He had hoped there would be a note or at least something obvious. He used the Omni as a magnifying glass and scanned the surface of the component, but found nothing. He then looked at the inside of the case. There was a small sticker with a serial number on it and an old-fashioned barcode. That was strange; barcodes were no longer used. He entered the codes in a search agent and instructed it to do a wide search, with a weighting towards locations. It came back within a second with a definite match on an item number. The barcode was genuine. It led to a product description of the memTag. He studied the barcode again, this time magnifying it. Buried in the black bars on the sticker were tiny numbers. At first he thought they matched the barcode, but comparing them side by side he noticed a few of the numbers were different. He took this new set of numbers and ran the agent again. This time a location came up with a high probability match. It was a church, of all things.

He sat back and as he did, images and patterns started flickering in his mind like an old TV set struggling to tune in a channel. He didn't have time for another episode. He tried to tell his glitching mind to stop, but his subconscious mind was too fascinated to let his conscious mind interrupt.

This was different from the previous episodes. He could still think and reason even if he was incapable of affecting anything. Before, he had blanked out completely. He studied the patterns bubbling in his mind: images from his childhood, advertisements, structured patterns such as fractals, and more outlandish patterns that seemed to describe touch, taste and smell. They made no sense, but his mind arranged, rearranged, stacked, overlapped and broke them apart in a desperate attempt to find order. Was this what it was like to be a deadhead? To be aware of your mind's futile attempts to make sense of the unrelated. He wasn't supposed to join their ranks yet, or at least not according to the projected timeline from his doctor, but maybe stress had brought it on early.

The images overwhelmed him and he tried to remove himself from the chaos. To his surprise, it worked. He found himself in absolute darkness. He could still feel his unconscious mind working away, trying to decipher the images, but it was a distant concern. Again he wondered if this was where deadheads ended up – hiding in a comforting darkness, away from the impressions of a disintegrating mind. Was he now stuck here, choosing only between darkness and a sensory onslaught?

He forced himself from the darkness, through the patterns and into the regular world. At first it was overwhelming, like an oversaturated photograph, but it slowly resolved itself into the sterile world of the research facility. This was yet another change. Previously he hadn't been able to consciously end an episode, but this revelation gave little comfort, as his head pounded from the effort.

He no longer had a choice. He could either remain here and turn into a vegetable over the next few days, or follow the breadcrumbs Adrian had left. It was a slim hope, but at least it was something.

He didn't know how long he had before another episode, so he went in search of TikTak. Tom didn't know how far their newfound friendship stretched, especially considering what he was going to ask of him, but he needed any help he could get where he was going.

Tom found him in the research room where Elize lay.

"TikTak? I need to tell you something."

"Is it about Adrian's audio files you've been listening to?"

"How did you know?"

"I overheard some of it. Don't worry, no one else knows."

"I have a location for Adrian."

"So? I wanted to find my father. I have. We even have Elize. Who cares about Adrian?"

"He can cure people who haven't turned. He can cure me."

"Why would he do that? Why you?"

"I don't know."

"You want us to walk into another trap?"

"Yes, it could be a trap, but I don't think we have a choice. As long as we have Elize, Leonid will chase us and Adrian is planning something. I think he wants to start a new race of posthumans."

"And you want to stop him or help him?"

"I want to see where it all ends."

TikTak sat quiet for a few seconds and then nodded.

"I think you're right. I want to see where this ends too."

They both looked at Elize. Tom knew she was listening to them even if she seemed to be in a fugue state. Her silence spoke volumes. She was happy with their decision, so they were playing into her plans too, whatever they were.

The door opened and the leader of the mercenaries entered.

"If you think your lone gunman will break you out, think again."

"Our what?" Tom asked.

"You've got someone coming for you. We have him pinned down on the upper level and another team is coming. He doesn't stand a chance."

Tom looked at TikTak, who shrugged in response.

"We don't have anyone coming. They're after Elize, not us."

"Don't leave this area."

"Can we get something to defend ourselves with?"

The mercenary looked TikTak up and down and then threw him his tactical baton.

"You can have your toy."

He left.

Tom's Omni started beeping. A private video feed was playing on the screen. It showed Marksman killing two mercenaries with brutal efficiency. The first was struck over the temple caving his skull in. The second one managed to deflect the first blow, but Marksman just kept raining blows against his hands and arms, breaking bones with every blow. The last blow struck the back of his neck, throwing his head backwards. He toppled, dead eyes staring at the ceiling.

"We need to leave. Now!"

22

The Anomaly

The consciousness known as Adrian sent his perception soaring through the nodes. He always had at least a hundred active nodes in his mind's extended network, and they in turn had at least ten backup nodes. Each node was woefully inadequate, as most of the processing power was required to keep the node functioning, but it was a numbers game. Every day another fifty or so nodes were added, and Adrian calculated that he'd pretty much reached the event horizon where his network could survive any external attack fifteen minutes ago. He was immortal or at least as close to it as you could be, not counting earth-destroying acts of God.

And of course there was a God. He himself was on his way to becoming one. After all, to paraphrase Arthur C. Clark: "Any sufficiently advanced life form is indistinguishable from God."

He had run the calculations and it was extremely improbable that he was the only being in the universe that had outgrown its base civilization. There were others like him, maybe even more advanced, and he longed to meet them. He had started exploring how to extend his reach beyond Earth, but right now there were more pressing concerns close to home.

He scanned the locations of each of the potentials. He no longer needed them as his contingency plan; however, they were still valuable. They could be repurposed. Some of them had already reached the end destination. Some had disappeared and others were on their way. Only one was not following the expected pattern. The private investigator was still far off, toiling away at some pointless quest. Tom was one of the most promising potentials, so he had saved him more than once already, but his value was diminishing by the minute as the network grew. He would still make a useful node, but not enough for Adrian to help him again.

Adrian felt a sliver of curiosity about what Tom was up to that was more important than the information on the sound files he had given him. He scanned the surrounding network and was surprised to find security that actually stopped him for a few seconds, but it was soon broken down to its core components and disposed of. He discovered an access point to the internal cameras and flicked through the feeds until he could see Tom in a medical facility. He scanned the company records and soon found a connection between this and PharmaCom. It was owned by Leonid March! If Adrian ever had an adversary, this was it. He had always been against everything Adrian stood for. Not that it mattered any longer, but Tom was obviously a lost cause if Leonid had captured him. The potential resource wastage to extract him wasn't worth the value he'd provide. Worse, he might have aligned himself with Leonid.

A hospital bed behind Tom drew his attention. He forced the camera to zoom in on the face. It was Elize. At least it was the body of Elize. How could she possibly be here? Last time he had seen her, she had been dead. At least he had thought so. The amount of energy passing through her would have turned her insides to sludge. Yet here she lay, in much better shape than she had been when he had left her. He tried to brush it off. The morbid fascination with her body he could understand, and any corpse could be made to look lifelike. There were professions specialising in it. His probability matrix had other ideas. It reacted immediately. The mere existence of her body was enough to throw his calculated plans into disarray. He had to do something about it. There was a low probability someone could discover how he had taken her beyond human, but it was still possible. There was an ever so much smaller possibility that Elize was still alive.

He scanned the network again, this time to locate any information about the status of Elize's body. He couldn't find any data at all, which was unlikely. Someone was storing it off net. All historical video feeds had also been removed, so he checked nearby cameras and could soon piece together the comings and goings. A team of mercenaries, employed by Leonid, had entered the building and had all been killed. Two of them had Omni implants with data upload to an encrypted infoDeposit. He cracked the encryption and found audio streams from the time they had entered.

After listening to what had happened, he had no doubts she was still alive, but at the same time it amused him she had to defend herself in such primitive ways. The probability matrix adjusted again; the likelihood of Elize being more than a nuisance was remote. She would still be useful to him, but if he wanted to get her, he'd have to go up against Leonid. He had always known he'd have to do that at some point, but he'd hoped to strike from a position of power and he wasn't there yet.

It was likely he no longer had that choice. Most scenarios led to some kind of confrontation with Leonid. The question was whether to show his strength now or let Leonid win a small battle now so he could prepare for the coming war. It all depended on the private investigator and his actions. In retrospect, the decision to include Tom in his plans had been a poor one. All other potentials had been vetted over months to ensure they were suitable. He could trace back the rash decision to two key factors: He had just been in the final battle with Elize, which had depleted his energy and also put him in a state of mind where anything was possible. The other factor was the private investigator's potential; none of the other had come close, and this in itself had been worth some risk.

Now it seemed Tom would be the cause of the next trigger. Adrian didn't doubt he'd win if he chose to, but he found it frustrating not to be able to influence the decisions leading there.

He turned inwards to his system, checking his nodes to make sure they were prepared for the imminent battle. He no longer had to manage the nodes. His mind had become layered as more and more tasks were automated within the distributed nodes. His active mind could roam the network or inhabit any of the single nodes if he wanted. His old body remained in the network, but he rarely returned to it. The automation allowed each node to manage the absolute necessities on its own.

Lately he had noticed degradation in some of the processing nodes. This was to be expected, but it frustrated him regardless. He'd soon reach a point where he no longer made a net gain from adding nodes, but only counteracted the level of degradation. He had theories for how to bypass this restriction, but for the time being he'd have to live with this imperfection.

He had automated a function to continuously scan his node network, searching for security issues and ensuring the discovery of weak links. Five of the nodes reported an anomaly. They were still operational, but the degradation had continued beyond expected utilization level. He had seen this on other nodes previously and had cut them from the network. This time he isolated one of them and ran diagnostics to determine what the problem was. He could see a large part of it had become dormant to the point of being useless as a node. It repeated any communication received, but did not act as a processing node any longer.

He couldn't determine the cause of the anomaly and found no way to access it, so he left it as it was, isolated from the rest of the network.

23

The Trap is Set

Tom and TikTak found Dr Tak in one of the sleep-studies rooms. He was pacing around the small room, talking to himself.

"Dad, we need to leave."

"This is all your fault." Dr Tak turned and pointed an accusing finger at TikTak.

"The posthumans? Leonid holding us captive? The guy who's coming for us? What exactly am I responsible for?"

"I should never have involved you! If you blame anyone, it should be Tom. He brought you Elize in the first place. Everything that's happening is because of them."

"Don't bring me into this," Tom said, holding up his hands. "I'm just an innocent bystander."

"Elize and I were perfectly fine here until you showed up," Dr Tak said, completely ignoring Tom.

"When I arrived she had just killed ten soldiers with her bare hands. Is that what you call ok?"

"We were fine. Both of you should leave. Elize and I will be fine."

Tom showed Dr Tak the video clip. "A very dangerous man is coming for us. He will kill us all if he finds us."

"Elize will protect me."

"He's coming to kill Elize."

"So did the soldiers. Elize and I will be fine."

He repeated it like a mantra. Tom had seen similar behaviour before, but mainly in addicts. His fixation was around Elize and her wellbeing, whilst completely ignoring his own.

"Elize told us she needed your help," Tom said.

TikTak frowned, but didn't say anything to the contrary.

"She spoke?" Dr Tak was already on his way from the room.

They followed him to the room where Elize lay on the bed as they had left her.

"She spoke?" he repeated, speaking to her more than to them.

"She wanted us to leave with her."

"I don't believe you. She still needs to heal."

"No, she asked us to take her with us."

Tom picked Elize up, or at least tried to. He was surprised how heavy she was. Her skin looked healthy, but it was rough to his touch. He also noticed that scales had started forming on her hairless skull.

"It's a trap," she said, and opened her eyes. They were almost completely black, as if the pupils had taken over most of the eyes.

Dr Tak jumped back, staring at her, then immediately started checking her vitals.

"What? Is there a trap here? Now?"

"Adrian, the location you are going to ... it is all a trap," said Elize.

"How could you possibly ..."

"I will come." She sat up on the bed and jumped down. Dr Tak hurried after her with a handheld scanner.

Tom just stared at her. He had no idea how she could possibly know anything about the location, but evidently she did. Every statement she made was a huge leap, as if she couldn't be bothered having the discussion that would lead to it.

"Marksman is coming for you," he said finally.

"I know. I let him in."

"You? Why?"

"So now would happen. We need to go."

She set off towards the door without waiting for them. They all scrambled to follow her. They hadn't had time to determine an escape route, and Tom at least was happy for Elize to take the lead. She strode slowly from the room and through the corridors. She was heading for the lifts to the upper floors. Behind them lights shut off, equipment turned on and doors remained open. Tom had no idea for what purpose, but guessed it was a stalling tactic.

They reached the lifts. One of them was already open and Elize entered. Tom, TikTak and Dr Tak joined her inside. Tom turned around, expecting the door to close, but nothing happened. Elize just stood there without moving. Tom and TikTak exchanged glances, but didn't say anything.

Five minutes later the doors finally closed and the lift travelled upwards. It stopped at the ground floor. The door opened. Two bodies lay on the ground. There was no blood, but the neck of one of them was at an odd angle. Marksman's victims.

Elize passed the bodies without giving them a second glance. They followed her through corridors to the back of the building and left through an emergency exit.

Over twenty cars stood outside in the parking lot in perfect symmetry. The cars all started at the same time. The group followed Elize into the closest one. The cars all drove off slowly, like a funeral procession.

"So what is this all about?" Tom asked Elize.

Elize didn't respond. She sat staring out through the window.

Tom asked again and waved his hand in front of her face.

A message beeped on his Omni:

Adrian will tell you. Don't disturb me again.

Dr Tak laughed. "It is quicker for her to send you a message than actually say the words."

Tom ignored Dr Tak's comment. Was this really the end of the road? It didn't feel like it to Tom as he sat there watching suburbia come to a lazy weekend morning start. He wondered how much longer humanity could fool itself into believing that the world it had created would remain much longer. IntelEz had been the saviour, the get-out-of-jail card that humanity had so sorely needed. When it had shown its true face, societies still tried to maintain their old habits, even though it was clear they were on the verge of collapse.

From Tom's point of view, this was its one redeeming quality. IntelEz had been the harbinger of a new age – just not the one humanity had hoped for.

24

Praise be Adrian

The church was a modern affair.

IntelEz had almost obliterated religion. The Drug provided a clarity of mind that left people with little need for the soothing effect religion had on a mind trying to deal with things beyond itself. However, when the backlash came, so did religion. The old ones had experienced a resurgence and new ones were appearing every day.

This church belonged to an offshoot of orthodox Christianity. Tom couldn't keep track of the differences between the groups, but in general they preached against any mind-altering drugs, and this included IntelEz. The posthumans – and Adrian in particular – were seen as the Antichrist.

There was no reason to be covert. Elize was with them and Adrian was expecting them. They couldn't be more visible if they tried.

The large arched doors opened and a middle-aged woman in white garb came to meet them. She held her hands out to them, smiling as she approached. Tom couldn't help but think of her as an angel come to deliver him from evil.

"Welcome to the church of Adrian," she said to them, and started shaking their hands one by one. "I am Marian and I will be your guide."

When it was Elize's turn, Tom noticed a slight hesitation from the garbed woman. Elize grabbed her hand and pulled her into an embrace as they were long lost friends. Tom smiled. It was the last thing he had expected from the distant posthuman. Marian immediately disentangled herself from Elize and was all smiles again.

She shook Tom's hand. "It is a great honour to meet the last of the potentials."

"One of the what?"

"The potentials. Adrian needed people he knew could pick up after him if he failed. You were the last one selected. And now that his great work is complete you will be elevated within his followers."

"So what is this great work?"

"Let me show you."

She led them into the church. The main hall was an open space, with most chairs and benches removed. One corner had been turned into a basic kitchen with large pots and pans, whilst the rest of the hall had people lying on makeshift bedding. There was a musty smell; body odours and food preparation smells intermingled. It reminded Tom of a homeless shelter.

They continued into the administration area. The offices had been transformed into basic operating theatres. In one of them, surgery was in progress.

"We are restoring humankind," the woman said. "Would you believe I was a deadhead only two months ago?" She pulled back her hair and showed a scar running along the edge of the hairline. "Adrian is restoring us, making us better. Connecting us."

"Connecting you? How?"

"Adrian, praise be his name, has opened up the path to enlightenment, to the next step of human evolution. We are no longer single atomic beings, living our lives disconnected and alone. We now share part of our consciousness. Our emotional state and thoughts are there for everyone."

"A hive mind?"

"Yes, as analogies go, it is acceptable. Praise be to Adrian."

Tom couldn't shake the feeling that the woman, for all her religious posturing, wasn't taking this seriously.

"Why did Adrian lead me here? What was the point of all of this?"

"Adrian started his great work over a year ago and has, during that time, located many different people who could take over after him. IntelEz doesn't work the same for everyone. Only a few can fulfil their true potential, and you are one of the few. Adrian discovered this and even though his plans were nearing completion, he decided to initiate you too. That was why he gave you the audio files. That is why you are here."

"So they were just a means to an end? Was any of that true?"

"Enough to get you here," she said with a cold smile.

"So what happens now?"

An explosion rocked the building.

"Come with me!" The woman led them to the back of the administration area. A hidden door opened as they approached, revealing stairs. On the way down they passed soldiers at the ready. Tom stopped counting after twenty. Their heads were shaven and they all had the same scar as the woman had.

"These are real soldiers," TikTak said.

"As opposed to fake ones?"

"No, I mean real soldiers, Special Forces, that kind of stuff. You can even see the tattoos on some of them."

Tom looked again. They stood ready without moving, not even acknowledging them as they descended the stairs.

The lower area had a large group room and many smaller rooms along a corridor and a full kitchen. If the area above had been a homeless shelter, this was a hospital. The large group room had been converted to a sleeping area, with hospital beds lining the perimeter of the room. The smaller rooms were proper operating theatres, with state-of-the-art medical equipment.

"What is this? The VIP area?"

"No, this is the real area. The one above is a diversion. There are many people like Leonid. People who would rather destroy this great work than try to understand it. If they are not threatened by it, maybe they'll leave us alone."

"So what happens if they discover this?"

"The war will start."

She said it with utter conviction. The woman wasn't just one of the troops. She was one of Adrian's inner circle. Maybe she too had been one of the potentials.

"Adrian asked me to ask you," Marian said. "Did you lead him here on purpose or not?"

"Who?"

"Leonid." She frowned. "You didn't know he was following you?"

"I thought Elize was dealing with that."

She shook her head and Elize, as usual, didn't contribute anything. She was walking behind them, but apart from that had not shown any sign of even knowing what was going on. She had guided them all to this situation, or at least Tom thought she had. So what were they doing here and what was Elize doing here?

The white garbed woman smiled. "I have something I need to attend to. If you remain here you should be fine."

Tom raised his eyebrows. "That was my plan all along."

She gave them a small bow and then left the room.

"There is something wrong here. I don't know what it is, but I don't buy it."

"So who's the bad guy? Leonid wants to wipe out the future of humankind. Surely this collective mind idea is a good thing? Creepy, but good?"

Tom turned to Elize who had stood silent for all this time. "What do you think?"

"All has not been revealed. Just keep us alive."

Another explosion, this time much closer.

The soldiers all headed upstairs and the garbed woman appeared again.

"Leonid had more extreme ideas than we estimated. I will remain here to ensure your safety."

"What are you going to do? Pray to Adrian?" TikTak readied himself next to the door.

Machine-gun fire echoed in the hall above as the two forces clashed. Then everything went quiet.

They stood there without moving, daring the silence to erupt in machine-gun fire and explosions, but nothing happened.

"The first wave was neutralised," the garbed woman said. "There are more coming."

"How could you possibly win this?" TikTak said from his position. "You have no strategic advantage at all. They can just blow the whole place up."

"He won't. He wants to see what we are doing here. He wants to capture Adrian."

"You seem awfully sure of that."

"You don't get to know your enemy by blowing them up."

"Most of human history would disagree with that statement. Leonid doesn't want to know Adrian. He wants to eradicate Adrian and his like from the world."

"Is that what he said?"

Tom nodded.

"And you believed him?"

Tom nodded again.

"He may want to kill the current posthumans, but eradicate?" She laughed to herself. "He wants to pick their corpses of all their secrets. He wants to create more posthumans, but in a controlled way. He wants to create a new super race reporting to *him*. Or maybe he wants to be posthuman himself. It doesn't really matter. He doesn't have the necessary traits for it, anyway. Surely what we are doing here is better."

"And what exactly is that?"

Marksman appeared in the door and immediately had to block a strike from TikTak.

25

The Next Posthuman

"This ends now.' TikTak said.

"The student takes on the master?" Marksman said, eyeing TikTak with an amused smile. "You're a code monkey, nothing more."

They circled each other, assessing each other's weaknesses. Tom knew what they were doing. Anything you could glean from your opponent at this point could be crucial to winning the fight. They had both been in life-and-death struggles in the past couple of days. If one of them had sustained an injury, it would be nearly impossible to hide it now. Even general fatigue affecting concentration could play a part in the outcome – if they were evenly matched, Tom reminded himself.

TikTak attacked, raining blows at different angles. All Marksman could do was walk backwards and defend. The strikes were so precise it looked to Tom like a pattern they had both practiced many times before. TikTak suddenly crouched down and flicked the baton out to strike Marksman's ankle. Marksman barely managed to get his foot out of the way.

"Playtime is over. My turn," Marksman said with a grin. He attacked and Tom immediately realised TikTak didn't stand a chance. Marksman's moved with a fluid grace, dealing blows both faster and harder than TikTak had.

The same thing must have occurred to Dr Tak who grabbed a nearby chair and ran towards Marksman who had his back turned. Dr Tak raised the chair and struck, but hit nothing but air. Marksman had ducked, and as he came up struck Dr Tak on the side of the neck.

TikTak's eyes widened as he saw his father fall down dead. It had given him a slight opening as Marksman had had to turn away from him to deal the killing blow. TikTak feinted high and then struck against his opponent's leg, aiming for the knee, but getting the shin. Marksman clamped his teeth in a grimace. TikTak unleashed another flurry of strikes. This time it didn't look practiced at all. They came high and low from all angles, taking shortcuts wherever possible, trading force for speed.

Marksman managed to deflect them, but some strikes came dangerously close. His legs were barely able to support him as he backed away. TikTak, perhaps sensing victory was close, pushed his advantage even further. Strike after strike, closer to connecting each time. He extended his reach to finish the fight.

That was what Marksman had been waiting for. Instead of backing away from the strike, he suddenly stepped forward, grabbed TikTak's right arm and attempted a hip throw. He had to use his injured leg as support and it buckled under the weight. They both fell to the ground.

TikTak was on top of Marksman and still held his baton. He grabbed the baton at both ends and forced it down to choke his opponent. Marksman had both his hands between the baton and his own throat. He let go with one hand and started striking over his own shoulder with fingers like a claw, aiming for TikTak's face. One of the fingers struck his eye and TikTak involuntarily relaxed his grip a little. That was all Marksman needed. He pushed forward again, this time getting enough leeway to free his head from the choke. He kept hold of Tik-Tak's right arm and rolled around into an arm bar, holding the arm between his legs and pushing his hips up as leverage. TikTak had nowhere to go. He tried to attack Marksman's injured leg with his free hand, but failed.

His arm snapped. Marksman grabbed his baton and from the lying position struck a vicious blow to TikTak's knee. He rolled backwards and stood up, looking around. TikTak lay on the ground groaning.

"I'll let you live. For now. I want you to see this." He looked around the room. "Anyone else?"

The sound of gunfire again echoed from the hall above. Marksman ignored it.

Tom looked back and forth between Marian and Elize. Neither of them made any move to come to TikTak's rescue. Tom knew he wouldn't last a second against Marksman without a weapon, so he shook his head.

Marksman limped over to where they stood, picking his baton up on the way.

"How do I become like you?" he asked Elize.

She didn't respond.

"Tell me!" Marksman raised the baton over his head, ready to strike.

Elize still didn't acknowledge his existence.

"Tell me, or I'll kill ..." Marksman stopped. Tom knew his dilemma. There was no way to intimidate her. Whatever he said next had to be real and enforced.

"Tell me, or I'll kill the private investigator."

"What do you mean?" Tom said. "Why would she care ..."

"What do you want?" Elize said, finally focusing on him.

Tom was surprised. Why would Elize have any interest in him? Why let Dr Tak die and TikTak be struck down, but stop him from being injured?

"How do I become like you?" he asked Elize.

She shook her head.

"I don't know how. Adrian does. He made me." She looked at the woman who had guided them, and who now stood in the door, her clothes bloody and torn.

"And where is he?" he asked the woman, aiming his gun at her.

"That is Adrian," Elize said.

"Busted," Marian said with a big grin.

"You're Adrian?" It was obvious Marksman didn't believe it.

The woman just smiled.

"You can swap bodies now?"

"Nothing so simple. You are looking at the edge of my network. I've become a distributed mind. Posthuman was only the first stage."

"So the hive mind and all that was a lie?" Tom asked.

"I told you what you needed to hear, but the hive analogy may still be apt. Who says the hive isn't just an extension of the will of the queen?"

TikTak sat up, cradling his shattered knee. "So you are using deadheads as processors where you are the operating system? What happens to the minds of the deadheads you take over?"

"They'd thank me for being part of the greatest leap in evolution ever seen."

"Stop this!" Marksman said. "I don't care about any of this. They were a means to an end, nothing more." He turned to Marian. "How do I become like you?"

"Become like me? That option is no longer available. You can become part of me."

"So all that about restoring humankind was a lie?"

"Of course not! I am the next step in the development of humankind. Every person will become a node in the network of my mind. It will be glorious." He beamed at them. "Praise be to Adrian."

"Fuck you," Marksman said and shot her.

She fell to the ground, without a sound. It was as if she'd been turned off.

"No, fuck *you*," three young soldiers, two male and one female, said in unison as they entered, weapons trained at Marksman. "You can't kill me."

"No, but I can," Elize said.

One of the young men turned towards her. "We could have been the future, you and I."

"You still don't understand," Elize said. "We are not the future. Not now. Humankind isn't ready for what we are. We prove it. There are only two of us and how much chaos have we caused? Humankind will survive this and become something else, maybe even what we are now, but not now. You can't just skip millions of years of evolution and think everything will be fine. For all our intellect, we are still driven by base instincts. Until that changes, nothing will be different. And that is why I will kill you now."

"You can't kill me."

"Oh but I can. I have already done it. I've been part of your network for a long time. You thought I was trying to kill you all this time. All I was doing was placing bio-agents on you to breach different parts of your network. What's the point of killing your body when your mind is distributed? I've infected major parts of your network. You are already dead – you just don't know it. I never waged this war against you because of what you did to my children and husband. I saw instantly the danger you were. I've been working to stop you ever since."

The young man stopped in his tracks for a few seconds, looking down at the ground.

***

Adrian assessed his network, finding anomalies across it. Small dormant parts of each node. Some of them had already begun blooming, killing off the node's ability to function within the network. This was her plan, disabling nodes and using them as replicators to recreate that state in nearby nodes. She'd made an organic virus that was shutting down his network one node at a time.

He had no idea how she had managed to infect it in the first place, but he could trace the final trigger to when she had hugged the physical aspect of one of his nodes in front of the church. That was why she had come. To complete her attack, she had to come in physical proximity to one of the nodes.

Not that it mattered. It didn't take long for him to devise a strengthening of the individual nodes to stop the dormant part from activating, but as the change replicated across his internal network, he knew the damage had already been done. Every single full replica of his consciousness had been compromised. Some as much as 30 percent. He would have to rebuild them, but it would take time, more time than he was willing to spend. He decided instead to wipe the affected parts of the network completely and trigger a clean replacement image of each affected node. This would allow each node to rebuild from scratch, eradicating the anomaly in the process. Then it was just a matter of copying a functional image from somewhere in the network. He watched as the replacement image spread across his network.

***

The young man looked up again and gave Elize a venomous stare.

"You've done nothing that can't be rebuilt. I've isolated the damage you've caused. It is nothing but a minor setback. I'm already rebuilding my network."

"I've been analysing your network from the inside since I came here – arrogant to think that no one would ever be in a position to attack you from the inside. There are so many security holes, even in your core network. I spent most of the time devising secondary attacks. I infected the clean replica you are now using to overwrite the infected nodes. After that I'm tearing your network apart!"

The young man smiled. "A final battle? So be it."

Elize's body went limp and she fell where she stood. The young man just started walking around aimlessly and then stopped, staring at the wall.

Tom studied the two combatants, again reminded how different they were. They no longer fought on the physical plane. Their bodies seemed an impediment to them, something to be shed once their mind could be sustained in another medium. He envied them. His quest was ending just as it had started – with a showdown between Adrian and Elize and him on the sidelines.

Adrian had wanted him here as a part of his plan, but now that Tom knew what that was, he was no longer interested. Becoming a part of someone else, losing his identity in another mind did not interest him. He'd rather die and be done with it. Becoming a deadhead wasn't something he wanted either. Apart from killing himself, there was only one other alternative, but at this point he didn't understand it. Elize wanted him alive. There had to be a reason, but what?

A steel grip around his neck reminded him there were other players still in this game. Marksman had grabbed him from behind and was choking him.

"I demand you make me a posthuman or I'll kill him."

It had worked before, but this time neither Adrian nor Elize reacted.

"So be it," Marksman said and Tom could feel the grip tightening, closing off the blood to his brain.

So death it was going to be. Tom closed his eyes, welcoming the grey fuzziness at the edge of his consciousness.

***

"Is this death?" Tom thought, his mind suspended in darkness.

A single light far away caught his attention. Was this the tunnel of light so common in near-death experiences? Would God appear and welcome him into Paradise? Would his daughter be there waiting for him? He focused on the light and willed himself to move towards it.

Nothing happened. He remained where he was as another light and then another appeared. At first they seemed random, but as they multiplied, thin strands of light connected them until what looked like a major city seen from above at night spread out below him.

It reminded him of the mind maps he could see when he was on IntelEz, except much more complex. He no longer tried to move. He knew he was the centre of this space – everything else would move. He willed the map to take him to the beginning, to that solitary dot he had first seen.

That dot represented his birth. All light surrounding him represented actions or decisions affecting him. Lines of varying colours and intensities led from that single dot to others, representing the probability.

He wanted to remain here to explore, but a distant pulsating light drew his attention. He travelled forward to now and studied the end of his life. To his surprise it didn't end. From the current time there was a decision point with only a ten-percent likelihood of death. The outgoing lines suggested many options. One in particular interested him, as it had a high probability and included a line that seemed to depart from the matrix altogether. He followed it and a new matrix opened. This time the nodes were no longer decision points in his life. They were codes that translated to locations, people and devices as he studied them. It was a network diagram based on what he could access. The first point was his own Omni and surrounding pathways showed numerous options. Some were direct; others linked with intermediate devices. The closest one was Marksman's Omni. It presented itself as an integrated device and allowed numerous options for access. After a few attempts, he managed to get basic access. He didn't know exactly how it happened, but it seemed many actions didn't require his conscious self to have actual knowledge. Much as he didn't worry about how to open and close his hand, he now didn't need to worry about how to negotiate networks or gain access to secure functions.

He accessed the visual feed and saw the back of his own head held close. Tom could see that he had gone limp and was likely only seconds away from passing out altogether. So he wasn't dead, just very close to it.

He remembered Elize's attack on Leonid's granddaughter. Maybe he could do the same thing. He tried to analyse the different options he had, but couldn't determine any obvious way to achieve it. Instead, he bypassed all safety switches, turned up the volume in the ear implants to dangerous levels, and sent a static noise whilst transmitting lightning flashes straight into the optical nerve. Marksman went rigid and Tom could see how his own body fell to the ground through Marksman's camera.

He disconnected from Marksman after setting the noise and visual feed on a loop. He returned to the darkness with his probability matrix in front of him. It was obvious that he was unconscious, but for some reason his consciousness could still operate, even though his body had shut down.

A pulsing sound followed by a flickering light announced his return to consciousness. His sensory input appeared, not as a mandate but just as a possible option – he could choose to remain within the probability matrix. Maybe he could discover other aspects, much as he had ventured into the networked world before. He decided his physical self might still be in danger, so he turned his mind to the sensory input.

He watched as TikTak dragged himself over to Marksman who was sitting down, trying to dig his ear implants out with a knife. TikTak struck him repeatedly with his baton until Marksman fell over dead.

Tom stood up. His first instinct was to help TikTak, but as he approached his friend, a multitude of options presented themselves. Only a few had TikTak as a useful component either in the short or long term. In his current state, TikTak was a liability and lessened Tom's chances of getting out alive. Other alternatives with a higher longer-term value were to bring Elize's body. It was likely her mind and body still shared a connection and her value far outweighed TikTak.

He took a step towards Elize and then shook his head. This was wrong. The alternatives his mind produced were correct, but only based on value to him. They did not care for friendship or take any form of emotional debt into account. TikTak had, after all, saved his life many times.

Tom grabbed TikTak and held him.

"We need to leave," he said.

"What happened?"

"Nothing," Tom said and laughed. "The two posthumans are still fighting and humankind is still falling apart, fighting for scraps from the master's table."

TikTak frowned. "Are you ok?"

"No, not really."

"So what do we do now?"

"We leave."

They made their way through the church. There were bodies everywhere. Some of Adrian's soldiers were walking around aimlessly. Some lay on the ground in foetal positions, alive but not much more.

As he navigated the room, dragging TikTak with him, he let his mind wander, analysing what had happened. It was obvious he was no longer Tom. Something – or someone – had triggered his change to posthuman. Based on the data he had, there was no obvious answer. It was unlikely to have occurred naturally, and the only other options were Adrian and Elize. He let a probability tree form in his mind, showing Adrian was the most likely trigger. He had been a safety precaution, someone to pick up the work from Adrian if he failed. Elize must have discovered this and protected him as a result. Maybe she too saw him as a safety precaution. If she failed, someone else had to deal with Adrian. Analysing all other options, he decided this was the most likely alternative by far. He was everyone's backup plan.

So now he had a choice. Go with Adrian, go with Elize, or just leave them to it and deal with the outcome.

This decision had to wait. He needed to get out of there. The doors lay twisted halfway across the room, leaving a gaping hole to the outside courtyard. TikTak pushed himself away, tentatively supporting himself on his injured leg.

"I can walk from here. You need to get Elize, her body, whatever. This isn't over."

Tom nodded, and as he headed back into the building a message blinked on his Omni and in his mind at the same time.

Help me kill Adrian.